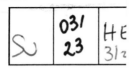

The Amusements

The Amusements

AINGEALA FLANNERY

PENGUIN BOOKS

PENGUIN BOOKS

UK | USA | Canada | Ireland | Australia
India | New Zealand | South Africa

Penguin Books is part of the Penguin Random House group of companies
whose addresses can be found at global.penguinrandomhouse.com.

First published by Sandycove 2022
Published in Penguin Books 2023
001

Copyright © Aingeala Flannery, 2022

The moral right of the author has been asserted

Printed and bound in Great Britain by Clays Ltd, Elcograf S.p.A.

The authorized representative in the EEA is Penguin Random House Ireland,
Morrison Chambers, 32 Nassau Street, Dublin D02 YH68

A CIP catalogue record for this book is available from the British Library

ISBN: 978–0–241–99494–8

For Senan Flannery

Ar scáth a chéile a mhaireann na daoine.

Author's Note

All characters and events in this novel are fictitious, and any resemblance to real persons, living or dead, is purely coincidental.

Contents

Tramore

(population: 6,101)

It was off-season and the local youngsters were up to no good in Tipp Phelan's caravan park. He wasn't about to begrudge them a few flagons in the dunes, until he got a phone call from the Garda sergeant telling him a 'bad element' was hanging around. Would he consider installing security cameras? Or a couple of Alsatians? That was the way with the guards, they'd make a suggestion and if you ignored it, you'd be done for tax or speeding or any old shite. The call would have to be acted on, but you were only courting trouble with dogs and cameras, so Tipp put a small ad in the *Irish Independent* instead.

WANTED:

Caretaker to live rent free by the sea

He was known as Tipperary because the only song he ever sang was 'Slievenamon' – in the back room of The Grand on a Saturday night. Nobody would deny he had a voice. There was a want in it that could only be understood by men, since it afflicted them alone. An unassailable scourge for which there was no end, or cure. Whenever he cleared his throat to sing, a

shutuptafuck swept over the bar. Hush, hush, hush all
the way down to the lounge. Tipp closed his eyes tight
against the silence, and began:

> Alone all alone by the wave-washed strand
> And alone in a crowded hall
> The hall it is gay and the waves they are grand
> But my heart is not here at all . . .

His real name was Michael Phelan, but nobody in
Tramore, apart from his wife Verona, knew it. She
called him Tipp anyway. And he called her Vee, or VP
when they were alone and she gave him *the look*, knowing it would drive him demented. They could be at it
half the night, and often they were. The next day, he'd
be addled with desire and a profound ache in his bones.
Early on in the marriage, when he was still hurling,
he'd sleep out of temptation's way in the spare room –
a measure he was forced to take after a bionic all-nighter
left him in ribbons for the county final. The sentiment
on the sideline was that he'd been 'brutal' and they took
him off at half-time. But the match was beyond salvation. Oh, Vee was lethal alright. At least she had been,
before the twins came along. These days, she was indif-
ferent to him, it was like living with a cat. When she
wasn't changing the babies, she was nursing them, one
on each nipple, their little fat legs kneading her stomach like it was dough. She was exhausted. Destroyed.

He begged her to patch things up with her mother,
'for the love of God'.

Verona bundled her breasts back into the sling she'd

taken to wearing in place of a bra, and zipped her fleece up to the chin. 'Hell will freeze over,' she said, 'before I talk to that bitch again.'

Twenty-two people applied for the caretaker job. Tipp ruled out seventeen immediately on the grounds of age, criminality and Englishness. Of the five that remained, four hung up when they heard the position was unpaid. The fifth was a musician from Dublin. His accent was thicker than tar.

'I could do with the headspace.'

The payphone swallowed another twenty pence on him.

'Do you know what I mean?'

Tipp knew exactly what he meant.

'The place is yours,' he said.

The musician arrived at the weekend with a hold-all over his shoulder and a guitar case in one hand. The other one he extended in a handshake that was too solid to be sincere, his dark eyes holding Tipp's gaze for longer than was necessary. Dáithí was his name and he was idling around the thirty mark, with matted brown hair and the makings of a ginger beard. He wore a hoop in one ear and scrap of black silk knotted around his throat – an affectation that left itself dangerously open to interpretation, but he had the strut of a man who wouldn't take any lip. They agreed if there was trouble he was to phone Tipp, and if there wasn't he was to leave him alone.

*

With the musician keeping an eye on the caravan park and the guards off his back, all Tipp had to worry about now was getting through the next few months without the comfort of Verona. Her plan was to dedicate herself body and soul to the twins, while he took care of the older child, a boy of almost four, who tornadoed around the house, taking swipes at balled-up socks and baby toys with a hurley that couldn't be prised from him. It was like a stick grafted on to the end of his chubby arm. He'd the energy of six children and the school wouldn't take him for another year, so there was nothing for it but to run him the length of the strand, until he surrendered to tiredness and fell asleep in his booster seat on the drive back home.

Tipp was pucking a tennis ball up and down the beach for the child the first time he saw the girl. She was walking arm in arm with the musician, her red hair aloft in the onshore wind. He watched them stride across the boulder bank in their long coats. At the dunes, the musician took the girl's hand and pulled her on to a sandbank. He held her hair between his fingers and kissed her face. A moment later, they vanished through a gap in the marram grass to continue their canoodling in the caravan park. Tipp imagined the girl lying on the faded candlewick bedspread, her skin lilac from the cold, her hair tangled and smelling of the sea.

The tide lapped its way up the shore. The child still had an hour, maybe two, of devilment in him. It was going to be a long night.

*

4

'He wants you to call down to the caravan. He has a form for you to sign.' Verona was crouched over a towel on the living room floor, a halo of frizz around her head. She had one baby by the heels, like a chicken, and was shaking powder on to its bottom. The other baby was bouncing up and down in a contraption they'd suspended from the door frame.

'What kind of a form?'

She handed him the rolled-up nappy. 'He didn't say.'

'Social welfare?'

Verona fastened the buttons on the Babygro and sighed. 'I suppose he has to live on something.'

Her breasts were loose beneath a peach pyjama top that had the words *Sweet Dreams* printed in silver across the front. He wondered what would happen if he touched her now. Would it hurt her? Would her milk seep out? And if it did, what would he feel? Arousal? Shame?

On the towel, the baby wriggled her arms and legs, she rolled over on to her front and scuttled across the floor.

'Tipp –'

'Yes, love?'

'Do me a favour and make sure you pick up all the Lego after you. I'm sick of standing on bits, and the babies could choke on it.'

The nappy felt heavy in his hand, he gave the plastic a gentle squeeze.

'I'm not getting at you,' she said.

'I know that.'

He walked into the kitchen and threw the nappy in the bin.

The caravan door swung open before he'd time to knock on it. The musician was in the process of replacing a broken guitar string. The place smelled of patchouli oil, cigarettes and, possibly, hash. He'd tacked a bedsheet to the ceiling of the caravan, creating a partition between the sleeping and eating quarters. Tipp could sense the girl was behind it.

'You have something that needs signing?'

'It's there on the worktop.' He held out a Biro. 'You cool with that?'

Tipp turned the burner down on a saucepan of spaghetti that was boiling over. He moved a half-cut onion aside, leaned on the chopping board, and signed the form.

'How are you enjoying the sea air?'

'Clears the cobwebs. Y'know what I mean?'

It was a peculiar habit Dublin people had. Asking questions they weren't interested in the answer to. Or questions for which there was no answer. Non-sensical questions.

Tipp was itching to comment on the bedsheet. The girl was so quiet behind it she might have been sleeping. Where were her clothes? And her boots? He glanced at the pile of blankets and coats on the dinette. 'I must drop you down a bottle of gas for the Superser,' he said, before stepping back out into the night.

The moon was huge above the dunes and there was a wintery nip in the air, but no wind, which was strange for the season. Hurricanes way over on the other side of the Atlantic sometimes brought almighty winds on their tail. Caravans would be blown around the place like Dinkies, tearing lumps off each other, you had to use storm straps and put a trough of water in the middle of the floor to weigh the chassis down. He eyed the caravans now in the moonlight, arranged in rows of three, dark and hunched like beasts in hibernation.

It felt as if the summer had never happened, and might not happen again. The non-stop checking in and out, 99s and the smell of suncream, kids who would at some point get lost and then be found, make-shift washing lines to dry their togs and towels. It was go-go-go until suddenly it stopped. In September, Verona went around gathering up all the broken spades and single flip-flops. She found a shit-stained pair of Speedos under a mattress in one caravan, and would not stop scouring until there wasn't so much as a hair clip left behind. When she finally peeled her rubber gloves off, Tipp threw them on to the rubbish trailer, then he hauled the big steel gate across the entrance and drove straight to the dump.

The girl was playing tricks on his mind. She was most vivid in the mornings when he awoke and took her to the shower with him. Sometimes she transformed into his wife, sometimes she just stayed herself and

7

sent him shuddering into ecstasy that he washed swiftly down the plughole. He wasn't sure whether or not it constituted infidelity. A less pragmatic woman might have taken issue with the amount of time he spent in the bathroom, or with his nocturnal discharges while she lay with her back to him. But not Verona. She moaned softly and turned to kiss him afterwards.

'Do you mind?' he'd ask her.

'Not in the slightest,' she'd reply.

Tipp considered himself blessed that she understood his carnal urges and did not read too much into them. Never trouble Trouble, she was apt to say, until Trouble troubles you. It was a good philosophy, if you asked him. Above all, he wouldn't have said or done anything to cause Verona pain.

The next time he saw the girl was outside the chipper. It was raining – lashing down – and he was in the car, waiting for a takeaway, when she came down the footpath, past the Bingo hall, towards him. She'd a carrier bag in each hand. They looked heavy. Was she doing the musician's shopping for him? That was the thing about starving artists – did the fuckers ever actually starve? After she passed, Tipp continued to watch her in the rear-view mirror, her hair hung down her back in a plait that swung from side to side as she walked. He imagined the musician's arms wrapped around her waist, the jut of her hip bones against him, the scent of her hair. Without a thought to consequence he turned the car around and took off down the Promenade until he caught up with her.

He rolled the window down. 'Do you want a lift?'

She stopped walking. 'What?'

'Can I give you a lift – to the caravan park?'

The girl tilted her head and squinted in the car window at him. 'Do I know you?'

There was a gap between her two front teeth. She was pretty as a kitten.

'I'm a friend of Dáithí's.'

She took a step back then and, glaring at him, she spat out, 'Weirdo!'

Before Tipp could say another word she'd turned and was gone down the slip. He watched her pound the cold grey strand and mount the boulder bank, up on to the dunes, where she vanished once more through the marram. Tipp drove back to the chipper to collect his takeaway. Whatever appetite he had was gone. The waft of vinegar from the bag on the passenger seat made him want to vomit.

It was pure contempt, the look she'd given him. But there was something else, something terrible in it. She was afraid of him. He'd frightened her.

The call from the guards came on a Saturday afternoon.

'You'd better go down to the station and talk to them,' Verona said. She'd been distracted by the twins and only caught the gist of what they'd said on the phone. A girl, a local girl, was missing and they wanted to talk to Tipp about the musician.

'Why?'

'She was seen with him.'

'When?'

Verona shrugged. 'Don't know.'

Tipp gnawed the inside of his cheek. 'Didn't she go home last night?'

'I already told you, I don't know.'

'So she stayed with him, what's that got to do with us?'

Verona put the cup she was holding down and studied him. 'Nobody's saying it has anything to do with us.' She folded her arms, or tried to, but her breasts got in the way. 'How do you know she stayed with him?'

'I don't,' Tipp said.

A patrol car was pulling away from the caravan park as he rounded the corner. He'd a cylinder of Calor Gas rolling around in the car boot, a delivery he'd planned to make when the time was opportune. Given the call from the guards, he was within his rights to show up unannounced.

The musician was standing in the doorway.

'Are you the cavalry?'

Tipp pushed past him, up the steps and into the caravan.

'Want to tell me what's going on?'

'Sure I'll tell you exactly what's going on – some young one has a bust-up with her ma and that makes me a fucken serial killer.'

'Is she here?'

'Didn't you see her leaving with the cops?'

He slid into the dinette and, picking what he needed from a bowl on the table, he began to roll a cigarette.

'Listen, Dáithí –'

'I know, I know, you don't need the grief. None of us do, man.' He lowered his head and lit the fag. 'Small town . . . small fucken minds.'

They sat in silence and watched his smoke rings drift and dissolve into the air. As he stubbed the butt, he let out a roar, '*Stell-ah!*'

Tipp tightened his grip on the table.

'Is that her name?'

'Yeah, Stella . . . star of the sea.'

'How old is she?'

'Sixteen.'

Tipp winced and then, imagining what he must have looked like to the musician, he winced again. 'Is that under age?'

'Dunno.'

On the way home from dropping the musician to the train station, Tipp stopped at the Jade Palace and picked up a sweet 'n' sour for himself and Verona. They ate it watching the television. Afterwards, they cleared the aluminium trays away and he did what he had to do to get the young lad to sleep, while she busied herself with 'The Twirls'.

His daughters were almost a year old and he still didn't call them by their names, because he couldn't tell one from the other, something he'd only recently admitted to Verona.

'Neither can I,' she'd replied. 'I'd be doing well if I got it right half the time.'

They were in bed when she finally mentioned the girl.

'So they found her?'

'Yeah.'

'And yer man is gone?'

'He is.'

Tipp could feel her eyes on him. If he turned to meet them, what would she see? What would he confess to? Gently, he ran his hand along the part of her body that was closest to him, his fingers remembering the soft curve of her thigh. He rested his hand on her stomach.

'Does it still hurt?'

'What?'

'The scar.'

'It's grand,' she said.

He closed his eyes and listened to her breathing beside him.

'Tipp,' she said.

He turned his face to hers and there in the lamp-light, she gave him the look.

Star of the Sea

I was in love with Stella Swaine. We met on our first day back to school after the summer holidays. By met, what I mean is *really* met. Of course, I already knew who she was. My brother Christy and his mates used to call her 'Stella Swoon'. She dropped her school bag at my feet, kicked it under the chair, and sat down beside me. Stella Swaine: kohl pencil circling her eyes, a silver stud in her nose, and lava-red hair flowing over her shoulders, all the way down the sleeves of her school jumper. Klimt's Danaë might as well have walked into the art room.

I could feel her take the measure of me. She flicked a glance at the floor, where my new Doc Martens were slowly murdering my feet.

'Are they ten-hole?'

'Yeah.'

'Cool.'

And that was the start of it all.

There's things you need to know about what it was like growing up in Tramore. Some unwritten rules:

Young ones from the estate are easier than young ones from the top town.

Stay away from townies and jackeens.

Don't go knacker drinking on the cliff top.

Stay away from the salt marsh, it's full of quick-sand and perverts.

Get out before you're twenty, or you'll have to abide by the rules forever.

This was the story for girls. Fellas didn't have to abide by any rules, a few digs was all they'd get if they stepped out of line. And whatever their transgression was, it'd have to be serious, criminal like, and they'd have to be caught red-handed. Robbing cars, breaking into houses, setting fire to gorse, smashing windows, hammering the shit out of the son of a local guard or county councillor. For any of these, they'd be flaked. You didn't have to do much if you were a girl to land yourself in trouble. Having a fanny was enough. Once you'd been cautioned, and you were cautioned many times, there was no good cribbing about the consequences.

There were degrees of consequence. Rumours would start. In school, people would mutter behind your back, but within earshot, about what a dirty bitch you were. Or a liar. Or a straip. Your talent for blow jobs would be scratched with Biro nibs into desks and toilet doors. Notes would circulate and find their way into your school bag, grubby scraps of copy book that diagnosed you with crabs. Around the town, people would stop talking to you because a teacher, or some-body's mam, cousin or next-door neighbour – basically any nosy parker with nothing better to do – had passed remarks about you. You'd be sent to Coventry, and there you'd stay until somebody popular decided you'd served your time, and you'd be let back in. From that day on you'd keep your head down.

Pregnancy was the ultimate consequence. We all knew this, because we were told (umpteen times) that it was a given for any girl who went gallivanting across the sand dunes, particularly in the company of a townie. They could knock you up just by looking at you. It happened to three girls from our school. Nicki Power, who'd a baby boy and ended up married to the brother of the young fella who got her into trouble. And Louise Hearne, who'd to be taken to Liverpool by her mam to get rid of it. When they got back, all the fellas pretended they didn't know her for fear they'd get the blame, even though the dogs in the street knew that Oscar Mulcahy was responsible. I swear, you'd have thought babies were contagious, the way everyone avoided her.

The one I knew best was Geraldine Halpin. I have this memory of her, after everybody had stopped talking to her, sitting against the handball court in her woollen socks and kilt, hairy white knees tucked up under chin. She was deep in conversation with Stella, who couldn't have given two shits on a Sunday what anybody thought, and in hindsight probably only attached herself to Ger because Stella was contrary like that. Geraldine Halpin was starting to show. She didn't come to school one morning, or the next, or the one after that, eventually the days turned into weeks, and the weeks ran into months until she vanished entirely from our minds.

In February, Thomas Power got expelled for boxing Frog Flynn, the principal, in the face and breaking his nose. Around Easter, Martina Kelly's father locked her mother and all the children into an upstairs bedroom and tried to set fire to the house. In June, the amusements opened for the season, and on the last day of school, we drank cider in the dunes and went down to the boating lake to hire pedalos that we rammed into each other until the owner roared at us that he was calling the guards if we didn't fuck off for ourselves. Nobody thought about Geraldine Halpin on the last day of school. The only proof she'd been one of us was a class photograph that hung in the corridor by the curate's office. There was her small blonde head, third from the left in the middle row. She'd blinked at the wrong moment and her eyes were closed.

Years later – when it was alright to wonder aloud, 'Whatever happened to Geraldine Halpin?' – I was told she'd gone to live with a relation in Cork, where she got a job in a meat processing plant that supplied all the big supermarkets with black and white pudding. She had a baby girl and called her Saoirse, the Irish for 'freedom'. My brother said it was because the Halpins were 'mad Republicans' and 'in the RA', but I reckon Ger had her own reasons for picking the name. It doesn't matter much now – and nobody ever remarked on it, either before or after she'd gone to

Cork – but Geraldine Halpin was an out-and-out brainbox.

So you see how it was, if a young one acted peculiar, the first thought to enter your head was that she was after getting herself into trouble. And that's what I thought about Stella Swaine the day she showed up in my art class. She'd a way of talking that told me she should have gone to the Ursulines to do her Leaving, and from there on to college. Stella was top town, yet here she was lumped in with the rest of us. Had she been sent to Liverpool over the summer? I imagined some randy yoke, with a stink off him, ogling and pawing at her, his hand clamped over her mouth and him huffing and puffing into her. I saw myself sneak up behind him and bash his head in with a rock. How invincible I felt afterwards when Stella, weeping with gratitude and relief, threw herself into my arms. You're grand, I whispered into her ear. It's going to be alright. She lay her head on my shoulder and I stroked her marvellous hair.

Miss Delahunt was at the top of the classroom, talking with great emphasis about what should and should not go into our Leaving Cert portfolios. I was a big fan of Miss Delahunt, but try as I might, I could not concentrate on what she was saying. Stella Swaine wore fishnet tights under her kilt, she smelled of patchouli oil and her fingernails were painted blue. She thought my new Docs were 'cool'. Miss Delahunt was looking down the room at me, like she was waiting for an answer.

'Are you listening, Helen?'

I nodded my head to assure her I was. Honest to God, I was.

It wasn't long before Stella and me were spending lunch break together. I'd eat Ritz crackers with cheese spread and she'd take noisy bites from an apple. We practised calligraphy, making black cursive swirls with our cartridge pens, filling the back pages of our copy books with song lyrics. Before the bell went, we'd go out behind the boiler house for a fag. Eventually, I worked up the nerve to ask her why she wasn't going to the Ursulines.

'Can't stand nuns.'

'Did your mam let you choose?'

'My mother is a bitch.' She exhaled a plume of smoke into the air. 'And a philistine.'

I could relate to this because my mother was also a bitch and a philistine.

Stella passed me the fag. She swept her hair up, tied it into a knot on top of her head, and stuck a pencil in it. Her mother was hoping she'd go to university to do something with prospects, like her sister, who was away studying 'communications'.

'According to Nancy, art college is a waste of time and money. So fuck her.'

I wasn't sure if Nancy was her sister or her mother. I told Stella my mam was of the exact same view, and not just about art college, about all colleges. I wouldn't be going. I'd do my Leaving and get a job. End of story.

'So fuck her too, because I'm going to college in Dublin.'

'Well, la-dee-fucken-da,' said Stella, and we both burst out laughing.

I passed the fag back to her. 'Maybe we could go to college together?'

'Yeah,' she said. 'We need to get out of this shit-hole.' She took a last drag and dropped the butt into a puddle. 'The two of us – like Bonnie and Clyde.'

I started a list of 'Reasons to Go to College':

1. To leave Tramore and NEVER come back.
2. To make Stella Swaine like me.

The third reason to go to college was something I didn't write down because it sounded big-headed. Like, who the fuck did I think I was? Deep down, I knew that I was good, *really* good, at art. Miss Delahunt knew it too. She kept on at me and it'd been on my mind all summer. I sketched on every bit of paper I could find: brown bags, half-filled copy books, dockets Da gave me from the builders' providers. I'd Nanny and Mam hounded not to throw away cereal boxes, because when you split them open the grey cardboard was the best thing to draw on with a pencil. It made my shading look like real art, something you might actually put up on a wall and not be embarrassed about. Now that Stella and me were friends, there wasn't a day I didn't fantasize about the two of us going to college together in Dublin. We'd share a flat and listen to The Cure on a loop. I wanted it with every lovesick bone in my body, but I'd to keep telling myself to cop on because it might not happen. And what would I do then?

The first time I drew her was at Halloween. There was a bonfire on the green and for days, Christy had been dragging wooden pallets into the backyard. He'd managed to get four bald tyres for the bonfire too. Da gave out and went to the pub. Mam said it was tradition. Herself and Nanny put on their coats and stood on the edge of the green, away from the sparks and the rubber fumes. They huddled under umbrellas with the other women, there to keep tabs on the cider consumption, in case the lads got out of hand or took turns jumping through the flames.

Stella and me watched from my bedroom window. She cracked monkey nuts and tossed them into her mouth. The carpet was covered with dust and shells. Mam'd have a conniption if they wound up in the Hoover. Every few minutes a banger exploded and there was a loud cheer from the crowd on the green.

'We should've gone to your house,' I said, all casual – like I was in her house morning, noon and night, when in fact, I'd never set foot in the place.

'Nah,' she said. 'It's more fun here.'

The flames rose higher. Their reflection danced on the windowpane, and softened Stella's features. Her eyes were close-set, her nose stopped a good inch short of her mouth, and there was a gap between her two front teeth. I studied the line of her jaw, the arch of her eyebrows, the dimple on her right cheek.

'What?' she said.

'What, what?' I said back.

'What are you gawking at?'

I hesitated.

'Can I draw you?'

'Sure.'

She started to take off her clothes.

'I meant a portrait – of your face.'

'Helen!'

'What?'

'Are you too much of a prude to draw me in the nude?'

'Of course not.'

Her dimple twitched. 'Maybe I should be the one drawing you.'

Heat raced up my neck. She was mocking me and I could feel myself blush. I lowered my head and rummaged in my pencil case.

'But you'd have to strip, take everything off.'

'Sure,' I said. 'Life drawing, the human form, we need to learn about it.'

Stella snorted and pulled her jumper up over her head. 'In holy Ireland, Helen? Dream on.' She pulled her leggings down. 'Next time, I'll draw you?'

'Yeah, sure.'

My hand shook as I sketched her, stretched out naked on my bed, with her face to the wall and her hair

streaming across the pillow. When the drawing was finished, I asked if she wanted to keep it. She glanced at
the page and told me to put it in my portfolio. Then she
picked her underwear off the floor and began to get
dressed. Her knickers were black. I tried not to look as
she put them on. Outside on the green, there was a *put-
put-put* as the lads set off fireworks, illegal spurts of red
and orange that shot up into the damp night. But no
amount of whooping and cheering would make them
take flight. One by one, the rockets fell. They died with
a hiss and littered the grass with soggy cartridges. I
stuffed the sketchbook under my mattress and hoped
to God my mother wouldn't find it.

In school they'd taken to calling us 'Hella'. It made my
heart skip whenever I heard it. Stella curled her lip. It
was 'moronic', she said. We started bunking off classes
and hanging around Newtown Pier, just the two of us,
rolling our own cigarettes with the storm wall shield-
ing us from a wind that was bent on blowing our
tobacco out to sea. Stella was better than I was at it. My
fingers stuck to the Rizla and dragged the delicate
paper until it tore. I'd manage, eventually, but my roll-
ups were either too tight to smoke, or too baggy, with
strands of Old Holborn poking out either end, ugly as
ear hair. I'd study Stella's hands. Like a magician, she'd
have two rolled in no time. One for herself and one for
me. She was beautiful down to her fingernails, and I
worshipped every unattainable inch of her.

Of course, she forgot she'd ever asked to draw me.

Dread gave way to relief as I filled my sketchbook with impressions of her, disembodied arms and legs, fingers and toes, and what I loved most of all: thick waves of hair cascading down her back, or woven into a braid between her shoulder blades. I called them all *The Muse* and numbered them. It was one of these I decided to show Miss Delahunt when she asked to see me about my portfolio.

She was standing on a chair in the art room, spelling out M-O-N-E-T by pressing thumbtacks into a corkboard, beneath which two dozen woeful attempts at waterlilies were pinned to the wall. I tapped on the glass. She turned, hopped on to the floor, and pocketed a handful of tacks in the front of her smock.

'*Tar isteach*,' she said. Come in.

Miss Delahunt was different to the other teachers. She always dressed in jeans and monkey boots. She wore feather and seashell earrings that looked homemade. Her spiky hair was dyed the colour of plums.

I bumped into her one day I was with Mam in town. 'Hi, Helen,' she said, with a flutter of her hand. I didn't know what to say. I just smiled as we passed.

'Who's that?' Mam asked.

'My art teacher.'

Mam tutted and said she looked like a right consequence. Miss Delahunt had notions. And because Mam didn't like her, I liked her even more. In fact, everyone in school liked Miss Delahunt, even the lads who nicknamed her 'Noddy' because she drove a two-tone Citroën Dyane. She was a good teacher. You didn't get the impression that she thought you were thick. What's more, she'd a soft spot for me, and sometimes asked if I'd stay late to help her rinse the sinks or wipe the tops of the paint pots before they went hard.

She gestured at the empty chair opposite her and I sat down, with my portfolio on my lap.

'Have you spoken to your parents about college?'

I shook my head.

'Are you going to talk to them?'

I fiddled with the zip on my portfolio case. 'Yeah, I suppose.'

'How's it coming along?'

I took the sketchpad from my case and slid *Muse no.8* across the desk. Miss Delahunt examined it and smiled. She asked me a load of questions. Had I enough pencils? (Yes.) Had I drawn many faces? (No.) She told me that faces were great for conveying character on account of the wrinkles and the lines. Expression around the eyes. The mouth, she said, was very revealing. What does it mean when lips are thin and tight? Are smiles always happy? I wondered if she was going on like this because I shouldn't be drawing nudes, or maybe because she thought *Muse no.8* was rubbish. I retrieved the page and slipped it back into my sketchpad. Miss Delahunt reached underneath her desk and pulled out a cardboard tube, like you'd put a poster in. She rolled it across the table to me.

'This is used Fabriano paper,' she said. 'You can draw on the clean side.'

'Thank you.'

'You know, Helen, you should have more confidence in your ability.'

'Thank you,' I said again. Mortified now and turning puce.

'Right, well, there's charcoal in there too. See how you get on.'

I cut the Fabriano paper into smaller sheets with a wallpaper scissors Mam kept in the third drawer, then I ironed them beneath a tea towel. The charcoal was dirty and tricky to use. You had to smudge and wipe and brush it as you went along. I practised doing sketches of our cat, Toby, who slept in the kitchen armchair when Da was in the pub. Mam'd be watching telly in the front room with my nanny, and Christy was always on a late shift in the arcade. I'd hours to myself, listening to music as I sketched the curve of the cat's spine, the whorl of his tail, the way he buried his head between his two front paws when he slept. Fur is harder to draw than you might think. I used white chalk for light, and a rubber to smooth out the hard lines.

One night, Nanny Moll came into the kitchen to make a fresh pot of tea for herself and Mam. She stood at my shoulder and watched me draw as she waited for the kettle to boil. She said the drawing of Toby was worth more than the cat himself.

'I'll give you ten pound for it.'

'It's not for sale.'

'Are you mad,' she said, 'turning your nose up at good money?'

I shrugged.

'Is it for your homework?'

I tried to explain about art college, but she just stared at me, for once in her life dumbstruck. Nanny hadn't a notion what an art portfolio was. I didn't want her to think I was being uppity, so I sprayed the drawing with hair lacquer and put it between two sheets of newspaper for her to take home.

Pressing the tenner into my hand, she said, 'I hope it stays fine for you, Helen.'

I was biding my time to bring college up again with Mam – but more seriously, this time. There'd be a palaver around interviews and forms, and we'd have to apply to the local authority for a grant. There'd be means testing, a whole lot of telling people your private business and maybe not getting anything out of them. I knew Da would say what he always said: do whatever makes you happy. Mam would say that was rich coming from him, given that he was only happy when he was drunk. She expected me to get a job. She worked as a supervisor in Darrers, Christy was in the arcades, and Da – even useless Da – had his job in the builders' providers. Why should I be any different? I'd be nearly eighteen leaving school. She'd left at fifteen, and Da when he was only twelve.

I rehearsed, over and over, what to say. I imagined what Mam would say back, and how I'd react. Because it was happening in my head, I'd control over who said what. The conversation always went differently in real life. It always ended in a row that I lost and Da was told to stay out of. The last time, it was so bad I half expected Mam to go up to the school and have it out with Frog Flynn about how the art teacher was after poisoning my brain, and I'd be branded forever with the shame of Miss Delahunt knowing something about my family that made her feel sorry for me.

On the Feast of the Immaculate Conception, Nanny Moll had a stroke. I remember because we'd the day off school. She was meant to go into town with Mam to order a turkey and a ham for Christmas. When she didn't show up, Mam walked across the green to her house and banged on the door, and because there was no answer she let herself in with the spare key. Nanny was unconscious in her nightdress on the bedroom floor. An ambulance took her away and Mam followed in a taxi with Nanny's false teeth in her coat pocket. I walked out the road to the builders' providers to break the news to Da that his mam had 'taken a turn'. I found him bagging sand out the back.

'What kind of a turn?' he said.

'A bad one.'

Was there any other kind? I supposed he couldn't just stand there looking at me with his mouth open, and nothing to say for himself. Da left drama to other people, and by other people what I mean is Mam and Nanny.

'And how is she?' He plunged the shovel blade into the sand and lifted a load.

'Dunno,' I said. 'She's in the hospital.'

If you were to ask me now, I'd say this was when things started to go wrong. But back then I didn't understand how families worked, how a malfunction in one part could banjax the whole apparatus. Which is exactly what happened after Nanny had the stroke. Not that I noticed, because at that time, I, Helen Grant, wannabe artist and probable lesbian, might as well have gone down to the dunes and jammed my head into the sand. I was away with the fairies, prepared to lop off an ear, or whatever appendage Stella Swaine demanded by way of human sacrifice. That's how determined I was to play Van Gogh to her Gauguin.

Mam thought Nanny was a goner when she found her on the carpet. I was kept out of school and we took turns sitting by her bed. One of the days, I came home from the hospital and found my school report beneath a pile of bills on the hall table. I ripped the envelope open, and there it was like a dig in the guts: 'B'. How could Miss Delahunt do this to me? I threw the report slip into the fire, and watched the paper curl up and turn to ash. Then I bawled until my eyelids were so swollen they wouldn't open.

See, there was something else. Something even worse than Nanny's stroke and the B in art. I'd been off school a week and Stella hadn't knocked in to see why. It was shocking how much I missed her, and how she didn't care. I could've been sick. I could've been dead. The thought of Stella Swaine falling out with me was torment. After another week of silence, she showed up on our doorstep, the picture of misery, and asked if we could go up to my room.

'The bitch is after grounding me. I can't stay long.' She climbed the stairs ahead of me, threw open the door to my room and flopped on to the bed. 'What's going on with you?'

'My nanny had a stroke.'

'Is she okay?'

'Dunno. That's how come I haven't been in school.'

'Me neither.'

'You haven't?'

'Nah,' she said. 'Stupid bloody report.'

'Jesus, how many subjects did you fail?'

'What makes you think I failed?'

'You're grounded, aren't you?'

'Helen, for fuck's sake, wise up. I'm not supposed to be in that shithole school.'

'What?'

'You said it yourself. I should've gone to the Ursulines. That's where Nancy thought I was going.'

'What?'

Stella rolled her eyes. 'I was supposed to change schools for the Leaving.'

'But didn't Frog Flynn –'

'Frog Flynn can't tell his arse from his elbow.'

I was trying my best to keep up. How had the nuns not missed her and called her mother? It just didn't make sense. I was confused – and it seemed like she wasn't telling me the truth – but mostly what I felt was relief that we were still friends, no matter what trouble she was in with her mam.

I dropped on to the beanbag in the corner. 'How did you not get caught?'

'Oh, who cares?' She pulled a tobacco pouch from her pocket and rummaged for the Rizla. 'I can't wait to get out of this kip.'

'Couldn't Nancy see you weren't wearing the uniform?'

'I got changed in Mackey's shed.'

'Marcus Mackey?'

'Yep,' she said, smirking now and looking at me like I was supposed to be impressed.

I wasn't. The Mackeys were savages who lived on top of each other in a mildewed pink bungalow on the backroad. There was an acre of land around the house, scattered with mangled clumps of machinery and broken-down cars, like a crash scene that nobody had bothered to clear. At the far end of the field was a work shed, where Marcus Mackey practised his heavy metal guitar and sold hash to local lads, including my brother. I used to see him on Friday nights, slobbering cunt-struck over young ones in the queue outside the hotel disco. I hated Marcus Mackey. And I expected Stella to hate him too.

'Why didn't you tell me?'

'If I'd told you, I'd have had to kill you.' She licked the Rizla and handed me the cigarette. 'I'm starting with the Ursulines in January. Nancy's after sweet-talking the nuns into taking me.'

'Does that mean we can't see each other any more?' Hearing the desperation in my voice made me cringe.

Stella blew smoke out the window and told me to get a grip. The heat of the room sucked the smoke back in, and rain splattered the glass. The endless gloom of midwinter sky hung above the rooftops. I wondered what it was like beyond the estate, down on the strand. That was true sky, with stars and the moon and outer space. But you couldn't go down and look up at it all. Not in the dark. It was the longest night of the year. People would say you were gone in the head.

'Maybe I'll knock in for you,' I said. 'Seeing as you're not allowed out.'

'Nah,' she said. 'Nancy'd go mental. Gimme your number and I'll phone you.'

I did a charcoal sketch of Stella that night, a profile of her face. She said it was a good likeness, but I knew that it wasn't. The neck was muscular, almost manly, and the line of her nose was too severe. It had nothing of her in it.

I signed my name and wrote our phone number on the back. 'You can have it,' I said, 'for Christmas.'

Stella leaned in and kissed me, soft and quick, on the lips. 'Thank you,' she said, and went away home.

Nobody had ever kissed me, never mind phoned the house looking for me before. Nobody ever called our house looking for anything. We'd a coin box in the hall that only rang when there was bad news for someone in the estate, or if it was a wrong number.

*

They let Nanny out of hospital on Christmas Eve and we spent the next day in her house. Mam made the dinner in our kitchen because everyone's oven is different and if you didn't have the run of it, you couldn't tell whether or not the turkey was cooked, and the last thing we needed was a dose of salmonella. Da and Christy were watching *Indiana Jones* in Nanny's front room while me and Mam set the kitchen table. Then we traipsed back and forth across the green with the turkey and the ham, the spuds and the sprouts, the gravy, the Christmas pudding, and presents wrapped in paper covered with holly and robins and snow-capped chimney stacks. Nanny took her dinner on a bed tray. Mam mashed the spuds and cut the meat into little pieces for her. I brought it up, put a serviette into the neck of her nightdress and sat with her as she ate, slow and bored. Everything went in and came out of the one corner of her mouth: fags, food and broken words. She was able to talk again, but hadn't much to say that was worth the effort. She ate a few spoonfuls, pulled the serviette off her chest and pointed towards the dressing table for her box of Superkings and her ashtray. I lit one for her, and one for myself.

Later, we sat around the front room unwrapping the presents: jumpers and socks, soap-on-a-rope and rainbow-coloured bath salts, a CD from my brother of a band that he liked and I didn't.

Mam was stuffing balls of torn wrapping paper into a black sack when Da said, 'Hang on now, there's one more thing.' He got up, and from behind Nanny's settee he pulled a fancy bag. 'It's for Helen,' he said.

I held the rope handles, peered inside and looked up at Da.

Mam was stood beside him, still holding the black sack, her mouth catching flies. 'Well,' she said, 'what is it?'

'It's a camera. A Polaroid Instamatic.'

'Right,' she huffed. 'I'll take off my apron so, and you can take a picture of us all.'

She'd a face on her that'd stop a clock. It was understandable, I suppose, given that Da never bought her anything. That Da spent his wages in the pub. That Da had been talking to me about something I hadn't been talking to her about. Given that the thing we'd been talking about was art.

We tried to get her to play cards with us, or to watch *Only Fools and Horses* on the telly, but she was having none of it, and spent the evening banging saucepans around in the sink, scouring every trace of Christmas from the roasting tins. I asked if I could help, but she hunted me, saying she'd be quicker doing it herself. I went back to the front room, where Christy was putting on his leather jacket to go up the town. Da was in the armchair, a glass of whiskey at his feet, laughing his head off at Del Boy Trotter. It was a pity I hadn't a sketchbook there to draw him. Maurice Grant, the only person on my side. I took a picture of him instead.

Mam stayed out with me about the camera. I think

she thought we'd been conspiring against her, me and Da. The honest truth was, nobody was more surprised than me by the present. But when I thought about it, I remembered how I was at the kitchen table one night, sketching the cat, when Da arrived home half-cut.

'Wouldn't that be easier to do if you'd a photo of the cat?' he said.

'But I'd need a camera and film, and I'd have to get it developed down in The Kiosk.'

'You would.'

'And if I didn't pay and collect the photos on time, Midge Maguire would stick them in the shop window under an "Unclaimed Photographs" sign for the whole town to see.'

Da said that was true. When he went to buy fags or the paper, there was often people gawking at the photos to see did they know anyone. It was only natural. He'd taken a look himself, and you were guaranteed to recognize someone looking the worse for wear. 'The thing you want,' he said, 'is one of them cameras that prints photos automatically.'

'An instamatic?'

'The very man.' And away he stumbled, down the hall, and up the stairs to bed.

I went back to school after Christmas, and Stella went to the Ursulines. I'd meet her off the bus most days and we'd go walking over the town towards her house. There were hardly any nuns in her new school, she said, and no boys either, which actually she preferred. 'No farts and BO.' She'd made a friend named Grace, who I'd get on great with. Grace lived in Passage, she'd a brother who was in a band, sometimes they played in Geoff's. I didn't know where Passage was – or, for that matter, Geoff's. But I supposed both were in Waterford and worth knowing about. 'New friend' Grace sounded like a bit of a dose – an opinion I kept to myself. That January, like every January, a sea mist hung above the town and it was dark by half past four. We'd say our goodbyes and I'd watch her walk away from me, then I'd take off down Gallwey's Hill, back to our estate, knowing that after tea Stella would phone, to tell me all the things we hadn't time to chew over earlier. I'd bite my tongue when she got to the part about Grace.

There was a lot of talk about Stella in school, admiration for the stroke she'd pulled on her mother. But the bitches had their say too, and since she was no longer around, they directed it at me. She was 'jumped up' and a 'weirdo'.

'What are you telling me for?' I'd say. 'Tell her.' Knowing full well they couldn't and that it was driving them spare. Stella Swaine had taken her first step away, soon she'd be rid of them entirely.

Though I wouldn't have admitted it at the time, I was able to concentrate better in art without her whispering into my ear or dabbing patchouli oil on her wrists. I was helping to clean the art room most days after school, killing time until Stella's bus arrived.

Miss Delahunt didn't comment on Stella's absence, and that disappointed me. We were her best students. If I vanished, would she not care about me either? She never let on, but I'm sure she knew that Stella was my Muse. I'd a feeling she didn't approve of me having a Muse, especially a naked one.

The camera, on the other hand, she most definitely approved of. 'How exciting!' she said, 'and what are you going to photograph?'

'People around the town.'

'This town? Tramore?'

What other town did she think I meant?

She heard me out, nodding along with the idea I had for my special project. Tramore was full of subjects, I'd take pictures of the people around the town, then I'd go down to the amusements and along the Promenade. 'My da says he'll even bring me to the races.'

'And you'll draw and paint portraits from the photos?'

'That's right,' I said. 'I'm going to call it *Greetings from Tramore*.'

Miss Delahunt thought my idea was 'super', and that was licence enough for me to take off around the town with my camera, asking people to pose for a picture. She even wrote a letter on school notepaper, describing me as 'a promising young artist' and explaining how I was working on my portfolio for college. I slipped this official-looking document into a plastic cover, and carried it as I went about the place recruiting subjects. It took some persuading but Stella agreed to come along. Her job was to set up the shot, to make sure the subjects held their position and that nobody walked in front of the camera while I was shooting.

Mam went ballistic when she found out. What was I at? People would think I was up to something, trying to diddle them out of money. There was a chancer who used to do that at dances, he'd take your picture without you knowing and then put the hard sell on you to buy it. That teacher of yours is a right article, she said. Oh, she'd known the minute my father brought that camera into the house that they'd rue the day. It was probably stolen property, she said, as if he'd ever set foot in a camera shop. He would in his eye. No. He got it for the price of a pint from some maggoty drunk down in Frank Tobin's pub. I was to stop, this instant, gallivanting up and down the town, making a show of myself.

She'd little to worry about because not a single person agreed to have their photo taken. It made no difference that I was in my school uniform with a letter from my teacher. Nobody thought I was trying to pull a fast one. They were just camera-shy, something I hadn't expected. Stella was no help, standing there with her arms folded, dispensing dirty looks like they were the height of fashion. 'I'm bored,' she'd say, or, 'this place is so depressing.' Sometimes she made excuses for not coming, she was too busy with school work, or she was over in Grace's.

I was almost ready to give up when the butcher Ted Burke asked to look at my sketchbook. It was, he said, a great thing for a young person to show such an interest in the town. Was he humouring me? Making fun of me? He must have been hacking a carcass in half before I arrived, because his white coat was all bloody where he'd wiped his hands, and the smell of raw meat was enough to turn your stomach.

As I went to leave, he said, 'If you give me a minute, I'll get cleaned up.'

To my mind, he was better the way he was. The bloodstains were dramatic. But considering he was my first subject, I was in no position to make demands.

The coat he reappeared in was pure white and stiff with starch. He'd a striped apron over it and a butcher's trilby cocked on the back of his head as he came bounding out from behind the counter. 'Might as well do it right,' he said, stopping at the window to twist a brass pole that lowered the awning.

I still have the photograph somewhere. He's standing outside his shop next to a six-foot plastic pig. Thaddeus Burke. Family Butcher. The happiest man in Ireland. As if he'd hit the big time when I walked through his door. He wouldn't hear of me leaving without two pounds of stewing beef. 'Give that to your mammy,' he said.

I thanked him and when I got halfway down the hill, I threw the white plastic bag of meat over a garden wall.

*

On St Patrick's Day, Stella and me were mooching around with the camera when she spotted a purple-nosed bagpiper sitting at the bus stop.

'How about him?'

I looked across the road. He was drinking a bottle of Bubble Up. Before I'd time to think about it, she tore over to talk to him. He nodded, she played with her hair, he nodded more, and then she called me over.

'This is Richie.'

He was got up in a green kilt and socks with white feathers sewn into the elastic.

'He's on his way to the parade in town,' said Stella, 'to play his pipes.'

Richie's brogues shone like enormous beetles on the potholed concrete. Beside them stood a battered suitcase, he caught me looking at it and said getting the bagpipes in and out was 'a major operation – and sure, the bus could be along any minute'. Stella took up position behind me and as I pressed the shutter, Richie raised his bottle, looked straight down the lens, and said, 'For Ireland!' as if it was a firing squad he was facing. A moment later, the bus came around the bend and I never got to show him the photo.

We must've been feeling inspired – or had some notion of ourselves – after that, because we kept on walking down to the Prom to see what else was going on. In the amusements car park, hawkers had set up stalls selling shamrock rosettes. They'd sticks of emerald rock, and disco-boppers with sparkly green love hearts on springs. Stella bought a pair and stuck them on her head. Then we stood against the sea wall, smoking. A row of tricolours flapped on the telegraph poles as a ghetto blaster, low on batteries, bleated rebel songs out the back of a HiAce van. Parked next to it was a caravan, the colour of a Super Split, with a woman sitting on a deckchair outside. She caught my eye and shouted over, did we want our fortunes told? Stella shouted back that we might, but she'd have to let us take her photo first.

'Ten pound each,' she croaked.

'We've only got five.'

The woman shook her head. But a few seconds later shouted across to us that five would do.

She wasn't one to take direction, so I photographed her as she was, spraddled on a deckchair, scowling at me. Soon as the picture slid out the end of the camera, she hoisted herself off the chair and up the caravan's steps. We followed her and ducked inside. It smelled of beef Cup-A-Soup and no matter where you looked, a holy picture or statue looked back at you with mournful eyes. There was barely enough room for the woman, never mind her three Children of Prague and the legion of holy water bottles she'd assembled, all of them in the shape of the Blessed Virgin with blue plastic screwcaps on their heads for crowns, except for the one with a gold crown, who looked like a baby bottle of Powers.

Stella nudged me. 'That's the extra-Virgin.'

The fortune teller muttered something and rested

her breasts on the arms of her blouse. 'Right,' she said, 'leaves or palm?'

There was a worn deck of Tarot cards on the table. I eyed them up.

'For a fiver?' she sniffed.

I'd never seen a Tarot in real life, and was mad to get a look at it.

'And in anyway, ye've to be over eighteen for the cards.'

Did we come across that gullible? I dropped my hand on to the table.

She took one look and said, 'You'll never get rich.' Her eyes narrowed. 'Or married.' She knew that, the minute she clapped eyes on me. 'You'll find love late,' she added, as if by consolation. Then, more bad tidings: somebody with the initial P would cause me trouble in life, and there was conflict coming down the line. Soon. 'You'll be stronger for it.' She turned my hand over, palm down on the table. 'Nothing too bad.'

A minute was all it took for her to spell out my future.

Stella's turn. She opened her hand like it was a revelation. The woman peered into it and said, 'You've the fingers of an artist.' She hummed and hawed. 'You're going to live in the sun, but you'll get tired of it, then you'll live in the rain. And that won't suit you either,' she tutted, and ran a yellow-stained finger across Stella's palm. 'The heart line is high.'

'What does that mean?'

'It's lucky.' She closed Stella's hand. 'But you're going to be in an accident.'

'What kind of accident?' said Stella, the sparkly green love hearts dancing on her head. 'When?'

The woman sighed. 'How do I know? But you'll be grand. Luck is on your side.' She stuffed the two fivers down the front of her blouse and nodded at the door. 'God bless.'

We sat on the ledge of the slip and I peeled back the plastic to look at her photo. It was rubbish. Whatever angle I'd taken it at, the sun was shining directly on to her face and the features were bleached out, overexposed. Five pound poorer, and bulling that I'd made such an amateur mistake, I told Stella I was calling it a day.

'Do you think it's crap?' she said.

'What?'

'Fortune-telling.'

'Of course it is.'

'Because she didn't tell you what you wanted to hear?'

'No, because it's not true.'

Stella wiggled her fingers. 'You're just jealous because I've got artist's hands.'

'Yeah, right. And you get to live in the sun.'

Stella leaned against me and whispered into my ear, 'Why don't you come live in the sun with me?'

Wasn't that the plan? I laughed and said I'd prefer to live in the rain.

'You're in the right place so.' She stood up and buttoned her coat.

'Where are you off to?'

'Into town.'

'For what?'

'I said I'd meet Grace after the parade.'

'Well, I might as well join you.' I took out the tenner I'd stashed in my coat pocket and flashed it at Stella. 'There's nothing to do here.'

She bit her lip. 'That could be a bit awkward.'

'Why?'

'She's only expecting me.'

The tide was retreating as I bombed down the strand, kicking at stones, raising clumps of seaweed with the toe of my boot. Fuck Grace and, well, fuck Stella too. For months it'd been 'Grace this' or 'Grace that', and not once did she ask me to go along with them. I cut across the dunes and around the caravan park to take the short cut into our estate.

Mam met me at the front door, and I knew by the cut of her that she'd been waiting. 'Inside. Now!' she barked.

I dropped my bag on the hall floor and trailed her into the kitchen.

'Nancy Swaine phoned here today.'

'Stella's mother?' A lump of something fleshy turned over inside me. 'For what?'

'To demand half her phone bill.'

'Why –'

Mam raised her hand to shut me up, then brought it down so hard on the draining board that the whole kitchen rattled. 'Sixty-six pound, she wants, for the yapping you've been doing all night, every night with her daughter. I told her we've the same problem with our own bill and that I've been on to Telecom Éireann about it.'

'But we don't get bills.'

She roared at me to be quiet, because she wasn't finished.

'That snooty bitch isn't to know we've a coin box. It's the last time she rings this house and talks to me like I'm shit on her shoe. And her rip of a daughter can stay away from here too.'

I could feel myself starting to cry. 'No, Mam, please. I'll pay back the money.'

'Are you deaf, Helen? Or maybe it's stupid you are. Stella Swaine is not welcome in this house.'

'But –'

'You heard me! And you may forget about art college. This photography nonsense ends now too.'

I screamed at her to fuck off, and before I'd time to sidestep her she slapped me, full force, across the face. Mam turned her back on me then and glared out the kitchen window into the backyard, where there was nothing but the coal shed to see.

'Get out,' she said, eventually.

And that's exactly what I did. I picked my bag off the hall floor and went to live with Nanny.

After Mam kicked me out, it suited everybody to have me living across the road. I was keeping an eye on Moll, bringing her up porridge in the morning and a mug of Complan at night. Somebody else – Mam or Da, I suppose – checked in on her while I was at school. Nanny didn't mind if Stella knocked in, but that was happening less since our mothers went to war. Another thing Nanny didn't mind was me drawing her. She'd be watching the black and white portable that Da put in her room. I'd twist the wire clothes hanger poking out the top this way and that, trying to improve the reception. She'd eventually run out of patience, flapping her hands and dribbling curses until I turned the bloody thing off. That was when I took to drawing her. Whether she was lying down or sitting up in the bed, she was always perfectly still, her face lopsided and stuck in an expression Miss Delahunt thought was 'peaceful' and 'wise', but she didn't know Nanny Moll. If you ask me, she looked like a melted candle.

I liked drawing her bedroom too. I'd no business there before she had the stroke, and you'd be in deep trouble if you so much as opened the door to peep inside. The rest of the house was almost identical to ours, but her bedroom looked like it belonged in another house. Where did she get the Persian rug? And beneath the net curtains sat a stool with a puckered velvet cushion and wooden paws for feet – where had that come from? On her dressing table, she kept a small collection of Belleek ornaments: china thimbles, a pill box, a cream and gold picture frame with dead Grandad holding up a fish inside it. Hanging above her bed, in a plastic frame, was my drawing of the cat.

Mam was glad to see the back of me, and I was glad to see the back of her. Da, on the other hand, started to take issue with this new arrangement. To his mind, we were just letting off steam, and it had gone on long enough. 'Tell her you're sorry,' he'd say. Or, 'There's a pair of you in it.' Wasn't it plain that I preferred the freedom of being across the road, heating pans of milk for Nanny and smoking fags beside her bed. I was fully prepared to sit it out until Mam agreed that I could go to art college, if my portfolio was accepted.

'There's a summer job going,' Da said, one evening he came over for his tea. Beans on toast and a couple of pork sausages I'd put under the grill.

'What kind of a job?' I knew straight off what he was at. Mam was all about people having jobs, and not being loafers.

'Dessie Fagan is looking for a checkout girl.'

'I don't want to work in a supermarket, Da.'

'You could put the money away in the Credit Union, you know, for college.'

Dessie Fagan was a brother of Paws Fagan who owned the builders' providers where Da worked.

'Why would Fagan give me a job?'

Da squirted a blob of brown sauce on to his plate. 'Why wouldn't he?'

I started at Fagan's supermarket the day after we got our summer holidays. It was grand. I'd half an hour for lunch, a blaa with whatever cold cut I wanted from the meat counter, and at the end of my shift, Dessie gave me a twenty-pound note into my hand.

'Why would anyone want to work in that hole?' Stella said when I told her about the job.

'If I save enough money, I'll be able to go to college.'

'But you'll be working for the whole summer.'

'It'll be worth it when I get out of this kip.'

She just shrugged and said, 'Suppose.'

After a month, I'd nearly three hundred quid put away and Mam and me were back on talking terms. No need for sorry or who's to blame. I moved home and one evening, when we were doing the washing-up, she asked me how much college would cost.

'Have you changed your mind?'

She dried her hands in the tea towel. 'We'll see how you get on,' was all she said.

I was at the register, putting messages into bags, when a customer stepped up to my checkout and dropped a punnet of strawberries on to the belt. She pointed at the *Helen* on my name badge.

'Is your name Grant?'

'It is.'

'Well,' she said, 'I'm Nancy Swaine.' She was tidy and blonde, with pearls dotted here and there about her.

'Hello,' I said.

Her face looked mean, I couldn't see Stella in it. Mrs Swaine had no more to say. She took her change without thanks, picked up the strawberries and over she marched to the sweet counter where Dessie Fagan was busy restocking chocolate bars. The next customer wanted a price check on a box of OMO, so I went off to do that and when I came back, Stella's mother was gone.

At the end of my shift, Dessie said he wouldn't need me the next day, after all, and would I ask my father to call in and see him.

'Righto,' I said, and away I strolled in the sunshine to Dooly's for a single of chips that I ate walking around the amusements. I settled on a bench by the bumper cars and took it all in: the smell of hot rubber and vinegar, the yelps of kiddies up over my head, spinning around with their legs dangling out of the chairoplanes.

The next morning, I was drawing in my bedroom when Da knocked on the door and asked could he talk to me for a minute.

'There's a problem,' he said, 'down in Fagan's. I think your friend's mother, that Mrs Swaine, is at it again.'

'At what?'

He closed the door behind him and leaned against it. 'Did you sell her daughter spirits?'

'Stella?'

'Now, don't lie to me, Helen.'

'No, I swear, Da, I didn't.'

'I didn't think so,' he said. 'Dessie Fagan doesn't really believe you did either. But it's her word against yours.'

'But I didn't do anything!'

'I'm telling you, Helen, that woman will make trouble for him.'

48

It was me, not Dessie, that Mrs Swaine had it in for. She was after finding an empty naggin of Southern Comfort in Stella's room with a Fagan's price sticker on it. Even a klepto of Stella's calibre couldn't have made it in behind the counter to take a bottle unnoticed, somebody must have bought it for her, and seeing as I was working there, the blame was pinned on me.

'Fagan's could lose their licence for under-age selling,' Da said. 'Or you could be had up for shoplifting.'

'Stella will tell her it's nothing to do with me.' No sooner had I said it than it dawned on me that Stella could profess my innocence all she liked, but she would never admit that we'd been getting drink from Marcus Mackey. If Mrs Swaine only knew where she'd been hiding her school uniform. Or had I been blamed for that too? I cupped my hands over my face.

'Dessie says he's sorry, Helen, but he has to let you go.' From between my fingers I could see Da sinking, as if the carpet was trying to swallow him. 'Yer woman could close him down. She has a brother-in-law a guard, did you know that?'

That's when I realized that people in the class of Fagan and Swaine could get away with things. They could make my father think he'd raised a thief.

Da must have been reading my mind, because he reached over and squeezed my arm. 'I know you didn't take it, Helen.'

'Let me talk to Stella. She'll tell them it wasn't me, and we can patch things up with the Fagans.'

*

When Nancy Swaine answered the phone, I felt my tongue go dry.

'Is Stella there? Please.'

She cleared her throat. 'Who's calling?'

'It's Helen, Mrs Swaine.'

There was a long pause, so long that I wondered if she was still there. 'Mrs Swaine?'

'You've some nerve,' she snapped.

'It wasn't me who bought the drink, Mrs Swaine.'

'It wasn't me who bought the drink,' she mimicked. 'Do you think I came in on the tide?'

'I swear, it wasn't. Stella will tell you. Can I talk to her, please?'

'She's not here.'

'When will she be home?'

'She's gone away with her friend.'

'Her friend? Do you mean Grace?'

'Yes, not that it's any of your business. Don't call this house again. Ever.'

'My father –'

The line went dead. Nancy Swaine was gone.

Paws Fagan gave Da his notice that September, and within a week he'd hired a Spaniard to replace him. Da got odd jobs about the place, laying tarmacadam driveways, clearing rubbish, working as a flagman on the road. He couldn't find full-time work, and it drove Mam spare.

It was cheaper to drink at home than in the pub, and since he wasn't much company, he preferred to sit over in Nanny's watching the telly with a bottle of whiskey between his feet. In the end, Da stayed in Moll's house, and Mam stayed in our house, their front doors facing each other across the green. Neither was willing to talk about the other. If you mentioned him to her, or her to him, they'd look at you in amazement, as if to say, 'I thought that fucker died years ago.'

Making Friends

Nancy Swaine needed a proper breakfast the morning they buried Vonnie Jacob. She was at the kitchen table, working on a boiled egg with a gadget she'd bought in Lidl. It resembled a surgical instrument: a scissors with vicious metal teeth that shot out suddenly and sliced the top off the egg. She released the steel jaws and noted the clean incision with a triumphalism not uncommon in frugal shoppers. The decapitated egg contained no shell fragments, which, though small and barely visible, could find their way into your mouth, and the crunch of shell against tooth would send a primordial shiver down your spine. It could ruin your breakfast entirely.

Behold! Nancy declared. The perfect googy!

It sat in a *Looney Tunes* egg cup that'd been in the press for thirty years, or more. It arrived one Easter Sunday morning, with a hollow chocolate egg, packaged in crinkly cellophane. She'd bought it for one of the children. Not Stella. No, certainly not her. Not Tish either, poor Tish was allergic to eggs. It must have been Michael. Christ, if they could hear her thoughts they'd have her in the nuthouse. Blathering on about a cartoon cat with a lisp. 'Sufferin' succotash!' he'd hiss when he failed for the umpteenth time to catch the yellow bird. She remembered the bird's name alright, it was Tweety. But she was flummoxed by the cat. Whatcha-ma-call-him, there now on a good china plate, with a slice of buttered turnover and a soft boiled egg between his two ears.

What do you think of that, Cat?

A silver spoon, and all. You're like a half Sir, so you are.

Nancy detested actual, living cats, and she wasn't gone on dogs either. Birds, she liked. Not canaries or parakeets or gaudy things with no business north of Gibraltar. Garden birds were her thing, waxwings and blackcaps. And the garden was her place. The garden was where she first encountered Vonnie Jacob. Nancy was bent over, pulling weeds from the rose bed, when two green rubber clogs appeared before her. Monstrous, amphibian things! She noted the slender brown ankles poking out of them. Her eyes climbed a pair of rolled-up denims, held at the hip by a worn leather belt and a buckle with some class of blue veiny stone in it. Unfolding herself was getting more troublesome by the day. Why on earth didn't she take the free kneeling pad they'd offered in Woodie's in exchange for her email address? Because Tish had warned her not to give out her email address. But what use was Tish now? What use were any of them? Now that she was rusted and calcified, incapable of greeting this unexpected visitor with more than a grunt.

Nancy jerked herself into an upright position. Her hand swung reflexively to the arthritic lump that had recently surfaced on the small of her back. A bone spur, no less! She rubbed it and tried to decipher the stranger: a lithe, tanned woman, with long silver hair, pulled into a bun on the top of her head. She was no spring chicken, but from the belt buckle up she was nothing short of glamorous; her linen shirt was the same turquoise blue as her eyes, a twisted rope of coral hung casually around her neck, and swinging from her ears were a pair of silver hoops. Nancy re-arranged her expression into a smile, which she hoped would be interpreted as 'welcome'. It paid to be friendly to blow-ins when you lived in a seaside town that couldn't wash its own face. The mods, the bikers, the stags and hens, the surfers and the sunburnt town-ies, between them they kept Tramore going, and always among them you'd come across a couple of continental strays, usually Dutch or German, who'd gone awry in their search for 'the hidden Ireland'. The woman in front of Nancy was clearly one of those.

'Are you lost?' she said.

'I'm your new neighbour,' Vonnie Jacob replied.

The *For Sale* sign was still up outside Tom Ryan's bungalow. Given how long she'd lived next door to the man, and what a good neighbour she'd been, Nancy was surprised nobody told her that his house had been sold.

'Oh,' she said. 'In that case, welcome to Tramore.'

In the weeks that followed, she saw a lot of Vonnie, who was 'desperate' to escape the unwelcome but necessary pageant of men she'd employed to get her new home into a condition she considered habitable. There was the man in a spacesuit whose job it was to get rid of the wasps' nest in her attic, the man to read the electricity meter, the man to take away the satellite dish, who was from the same company but was not the same man as the one who'd be coming 'eventually' to connect Vonnie's broadband. Francis Barron came to drain her oil tank, and left with a flea in his ear.

'The sooner the gas pipe gets extended up the town the better,' she'd grumbled.

This, and plenty more besides, was discussed that summer over pots of tea on Nancy's patio. Sometimes Nancy had to shout at Vonnie to be heard above the din of the workmen, especially the gardeners, a squadron of muscular men in stained T-shirts who spoke a gruff, mangled language that she presumed was Polish. They brought chainsaws and enormous electric strimmers; they could have felled a forest, or committed genocide with the machinery they had. At the end of each day a young lad appeared in a battered silver estate car, dragging an empty trailer, into which the men crammed branches and thorny clumps of sceach to be transported to the dump. Their tools were piled into the boot, and one by one they got into the car. It hardly seemed possible that the car had so much room.

Still, Nancy was glad of the commotion. It would be quiet soon enough. The tourists would go back to work and the children back to school, the amusements would be boarded up and the parking warden, with her nylon tabard and paper ticket book, would disappear from the Promenade. The end of the season reminded Nancy of the winter that lay ahead, and she avoided going down the town. There would be a week to watch the swallows migrate, then a fortnight about the garden, picking apples and wrapping them in sheets of old newspaper. The trick was to catch them before they fell on to the ground, bruised their skin and were spoilt. After the apples came the equilux, and then the days would shorten until there was hardly any light at all. A yellow fog would roll in off the sea in the morning and hang above the town, making the church spires look creepy and obscure. Nancy would cook a chop, or make a sandwich, which she'd eat watching the six o'clock news, followed by the soaps. At nine o'clock, the news came on again. After the weather forecast, she would turn off the television, set the burglar alarm, and go to bed.

That's how it went before Vonnie arrived – or BV, as Tish's husband Marty called it.

'It's nice to have the company,' he said.

'It is,' Nancy agreed.

'Better than living next to old Tom Ryan.'

She supposed Tish and Marty were relieved they didn't have to bother so much about her.

They were an unlikely pair: Vonnie, who'd cultivated a kind of bohemian chic that involved a degree of cross-dressing, and eternally taupe Nancy in her stretch-fit pants, little pearls peeping out from beneath her ash-blonde bob. Vonnie didn't take milk in her tea. She didn't do the Lotto. She could not abide television and, in particular, soap operas that were full of 'hams' and 'vaudevillians' who hadn't the talent for the stage. If it existed, Vonnie Jacob had an opinion on it. Coastal erosion, the migrant crisis, the Irish language. Mostly, Nancy was entertained by her guff, but it could be exhausting on days you mightn't be in the mood for a diatribe against the 'imbecile' who'd stitched the tricolour back to front and placed it at the entrance to the new primary school where it flapped proudly in the breeze, the flag of Ivory Coast. Her rants came in short bursts and concluded with a clap that sent the silver bracelets jangling like Sanctus bells up and down her arms.

'Now,' she'd say brightly, 'will we have more tea?'

'Vonnie's Vexations' Marty called them. Since Tish was working weekends, he'd show up every Sunday and Nancy would update him on the latest situations to discombobulate her oddball neighbour. 'Wait until I tell you,' she'd say. And he'd cock an ear, his lips already twitching with the start of a smile.

One afternoon, as they were driving along the Copper Coast to Dungarvan for a carvery lunch, Nancy announced, 'She's back protesting to save the wild goats.'

'Vonnie?'

'Who else?'

'I heard the guards were over in Bilberry looking for poachers.'

'Well now,' said Nancy, 'there's a cheesemaker above in Kilkenny – a German, according to Vonnie, with two wives and a dozen children – and he's after the goats. He wants their milk to make "Bilberry" cheese. She has her eye on him.'

'Go on,' said Marty.

'She's up to high-do on account of the fact that she's related by marriage to them.'

'To the Germans?'

'To the goats!' Christ, but Marty was an awful simpleton. 'The goats came with the Huguenots – and weren't the Jacobs originally Huguenots?'

'Quakers, actually.'

'Same difference,' Nancy sniffed.

'Right,' said Marty, 'so she has a prior claim on them?'

'She says they belong to the people of Waterford.'

Marty appeared to be digesting this information as he overtook a couple of continentals in a rental car, driving at a dangerously slow speed along the winding cliff road. He pulled back in. The road was clear in front of them.

'What if the German lived in Waterford and not Kilkenny, could he lay claim to the goats then?'

Nancy ignored him and continued. 'So, I gave her a lift into town yesterday for the protest. You can only imagine the do-gooders and hippies that were at it.'

'Did you go?'

She slapped his knee. 'I did in my eye. But when I stopped on the quay what did Vonnie do, only leap out of the car and into the traffic!'

'Jesus,' said Marty.

'And then, didn't she stand in the middle of the road and open her windbreaker like a flasher. She had on her a skin-tight T-shirt that said: "PULL AN UDDER NANNY".'

Marty turned to look at Nancy, and in that moment of distraction, a second or two was all it was, a tanker came around the bend. It was headed straight for them with its horn blaring. Marty turned the wheel too sharply. The car swerved off the asphalt and skidded along the gravel on the roadside. Nancy shrieked. Briars and branches clattered and snapped against the windscreen as the truck tore past them. Somehow, he managed to straighten the car and guide it back on to the road, but he was shaking so violently his feet slipped off the pedals and his hands couldn't grip the steering wheel. After a few hundred yards, he let the car drift slowly on to a grass verge, and got out. In the mirror Nancy watched him vomit into the ditch. There was a sour smell when he got back into the car.

'Sorry,' he said.

Neither of them was in the mood for a carvery when they got to Dungarvan. Nancy pushed the cabbage around her plate and tormented the corned beef with her fork. Marty managed a single potato before covering the uneaten food with his serviette.

'I don't suppose we'll have dessert,' he said.

'No,' Nancy replied.

They drove back to Tramore in silence. She didn't ask him in for a cup of tea, or wave as he reversed out the driveway, bunches of brome grass still poking out of the car's front grille. He could have killed them both, for God's sake. He was useless in an emergency, Marty. He always lost his nerve.

That evening he sent her a text.

– Hope you're OK?

Nancy put on her pyjamas and got into bed. She was jittery after their near miss with the ditch, beyond which lay eternity and all manner of possibilities: the pearly gates, the hobs of hell, salvation and damnation, reunion and rebuttal. Her husband Paddy Swaine, on his high horse, wagging a finger at her. Maybe in the end there would just be an infinite expanse of nothingness. Her mind could go around in circles all night. She took a Zimovane, laid her cheek on the cool, smooth pillow, and as she waited for sleep she wondered: how did Tish put up with Marty at all?

Nancy kept these thoughts to herself, for fear she'd be left on her own every Sunday. That said, there was no denying Tish had married beneath the Swaines. Nancy lamented this fact to Vonnie, one afternoon they were out on the patio, drinking a jug of elderflower cordial that Vonnie had brought over.

'He's a harmless sort,' she said, 'but Tish could have done better.'

'And what about the younger girl?'

'Stella?'

'Yes.' Vonnie took a sip of cordial.

'She's on her travels again,' Nancy huffed. 'In London now, would you believe?'

Vonnie frowned. 'Oh, I thought it was New York?'

Her interest in Stella bordered on nosiness. 'Well,' said Nancy. 'I'll see more of her in London. And of course, Michael keeps inviting me over to Canada.'

'That's exciting,' said Vonnie.

Is it? Nancy wondered. Perhaps to somebody like Vonnie. Yes, she could imagine Vonnie cutting a dash in Moose Jaw, Saskatchewan. Nancy had been there once. What a godforsaken tundra! And Michael's wife Winona was some piece of work. She exposed her breasts at every opportunity, inviting the child, even though it had teeth and was able to walk, to climb up on to her lap and gorge on her. It was obscene the way she'd spread herself across the sofa and smirked at Nancy, daring her to say something. She couldn't wait to get out of there. And no, she would not be going back to see the new baby. Let them come to her. Except, she knew they never would, despite being told they were more than welcome.

Nancy took a greedy slug of Vonnie's cordial. It was so delicious and refreshing, she must have already swallowed a full cloudy pint of it. As she twisted into a more comfortable position on the lounger, Nancy felt a sudden need to pass water. How alarming that her bladder could fill this quickly and to such a state that she could readily imagine a torrent of warm urine pouring down her linen pant legs if she didn't go to the toilet immediately. She excused herself and made a dash for the guest bathroom.

Vonnie was ready to leave when Nancy got back.

She'd her little knapsack in one hand, and the empty cordial jug in the other.

'You're going?'

'Oh, yes,' Vonnie replied. 'There's yoga in the community centre. Why don't you come?'

Nancy declined.

Vonnie smiled tightly and exhaled.

Once she was gone, Nancy opened the button on her trousers, kicked off her FitFlops, and stretched out on the lounger. She closed her eyes and let the sun's warmth seep into her, willing it to loosen the stiffness in her joints.

Autumn drifted into winter, and it wasn't unusual for Vonnie's electric-blue raincoat to appear through the morning fog, and there she was in her suede fedora, ready for action, whereas Nancy might, or might not, have bothered changing out of her dressing gown. This seemed to disappoint Vonnie, who'd already have been down to the Guillamene for a swim, impervious as she was to decrepitude. 'Use it or lose it' was one of her favourite sayings. 'Get your skates on, Nancy,' she'd chime, 'we're going for a spin.' And for want of something better to do, Nancy tagged along.

Drive to the bottle bank. Get a key cut. Buy orthopaedic insoles for Vonnie's expensive leather clogs. Attend a public meeting about flood defences. Vonnie Jacob had things to do and places to be. When she didn't have a pressing appointment, they convened at Café Caruso, where Nancy developed a taste for foamy cappuccinos, a habit Vonnie disapproved of. 'Fattening. And a stimulant!' she'd remark, as Nancy took the first delicious sip.

On mild days, if the tide happened to be out, they took long walks along the strand during which Vonnie was prone to reminiscence about her late husband Jim. He had worked for the local authority, and on account of that she maintained a particular interest in planning decisions. From this sliver of information, Nancy understood that Jim Jacob had been a person of consequence. She struggled to conceal her admiration when Vonnie spoke about how they'd lived in her husband's childhood home, a fine house on the South Parade in Waterford that had been in his family for five generations. It wasn't clear to Nancy if Vonnie was boasting or merely stating facts when she'd remarked that the house was too big and impossible to heat, with 'oh so many flights of stairs to vacuum'. Vonnie had waited a couple of years after he died, and since they'd no children of their own, and no relations eager to take on 'a heritage home with a broken fanlight and rotting sash windows', she decided, with great reluctance, to 'downsize'.

One morning, they were at their usual table in Café Caruso, when, quite out of the blue, Vonnie took a coughing fit. She rummaged in her knapsack and produced a cloth handkerchief, into which she blew her nose, twice. She stuffed the hanky up the sleeve of her body warmer, where it stuck out like a pair of hastily concealed knickers.

'Oh my poor Jimmy!' she groaned.

The owner of the café, Oliver Forte, had just arrived with their order. He was a homosexual and therefore emotionally astute. Nancy was amazed by his speed and discretion; within seconds, the teapot, cups and saucers, even the milk and nibbles, were off the tray. He spun away from the table.

Vonnie was still going. Tears streamed down her cheeks, she whipped the hanky out again and turned to Nancy. 'He's still the first and last thing I think about.' Beneath her tan and her spangles, Vonnie suddenly looked haggard. 'You don't know how lucky you are. If only we'd had a child, I could have kept a part of him.' She grabbed hold of Nancy's hand and began to squeeze it like a sponge. 'Tell me it gets easier with time.'

Clamped to Vonnie in this fashion, all Nancy could think about was ending the spectacle. How could she make it stop?

She patted the bony hand. 'Ah, now,' she said. 'Ah, now.' Then, she moved it cautiously away from her.

The fingers were brown and brittle as twigs. Nancy imagined them snapping off into a little mound of kindling as she deposited the hand back on the table, where their tea was growing cold.

In all the time they'd been living next door to each other, Nancy had yet to get a glimpse inside Vonnie's house. Once the workmen left, she'd expected an invitation to marvel at how Tom Ryan's dilapidated bungalow had been transformed. But no invitation was forthcoming. With the passing weeks, Nancy's curiosity turned to umbrage, which is precisely what she felt when Vonnie finally sent her a text message.

– *Come over for soup.*

Soup! If you don't mind.

The door was ajar when Nancy arrived. She pressed the bell, and Vonnie sang, 'Come in, come in!' from a distant corner of the house. 'Be with you in a tick.' Stepping over the threshold and into the hall, Nancy detected an unpleasant odour that she quickly identified as the ghost of Tom Ryan's cat. She opened the door into the parlour and was astonished to find it cluttered with twenty or more large cardboard boxes. Some of them had been ripped open. They were filled with books and what she presumed to be bric-a-brac, wrapped in brown kraft paper. A wicker basket stuffed with balls of wool spewed green and purple yarn across the floorboards. She wondered what the workmen had spent so much time doing. Rewiring? Plumbing? The windows were certainly new, and the wallpaper had been stripped, but the paint looked like undercoat. There wasn't so much as a carpet in the place, just a rug slumped over a worn leather sofa, and curled up in the middle of it was Tom Ryan's mangy cat.

'Shoo!' Nancy cried. 'Get out. Get out! Shoo!'

Vonnie poked her head around the French doors. 'You've met Mister Pickles, then?'

'Who?' Nancy's face was flushed with irritation.

'The house cat, Mister Pickles. There's no point

shouting at him. The poor thing is deaf, he won't go outside, it's self-preservation, I'm sure.'

Looking askance at the cat, Nancy followed Vonnie through the breakfast room and into the kitchen. She was dismayed to see her using the old Raeburn that Tom Ryan had fried his rashers and pudding on. And there, filled with small sooty pieces of coal, was Tom Ryan's galvanized bucket!

Vonnie was only just back from her sea swim and was 'famished'. She was dressed in some class of kimono, a jazzy number tied at the waist. Her freshly washed hair hung down her back, the damp ends of it dangling just shy of the belt. Not wanting to pay too much notice, Nancy shifted her gaze to the middle of the table, where a pink geranium was slowly dying. She pressed a finger into the crusty soil – as she suspected, a fungus.

On to the table Vonnie placed a chopping board, with four slices of soda bread and two foil portions of butter she'd pilfered from Café Caruso.

'What's on the menu?' asked Nancy.

'Oxtail soup. The craft butcher –'

'Ted Burke?'

'Yes. Thaddeus. He gives me a cut of oxtail, and sometimes a calf's liver, when I buy a chicken.'

'Oxtail?' said Nancy. 'In that case I'll take just a little.'

The soup bubbled on the stovetop. It fogged the kitchen window and filled the room with an endocrinal aroma that made Nancy's stomach lurch. She buttered a slice of soda bread and quickly took a bite. Vonnie's cutlery was heavy and hallmarked, the kind that required polishing. It had been allowed to tarnish. No doubt her silver cloth was buried in one of the cardboard boxes.

'You've still unpacking to do?'

Vonnie dropped her head to meet the lip of a spoon that was so gigantic in her hand it made her look like a child. 'Yes,' she said. 'I don't know why I've resisted, but I have.'

'Well,' said Nancy, 'I could help you unpack.'

'Oh no! Such a boring job, sorting through all that rubbish.'

'It's no trouble.'

But Vonnie wouldn't hear of it. 'And anyway,' she said, 'my nephew Ben Jacob is coming from Dublin next month to go through it all.'

'Your nephew?'

'Yes. He's a film-maker. He's going to make a documentary about the Bilberry goats.'

'Bully for you,' said Nancy.

In December, there was snow. It stuck and it drifted, and people were amazed to see the beach with a frosting that lasted as long as it took the tide to turn and wash over it. This was such an unusual event for Tramore that even Michael in Saskatchewan heard about it. He phoned Nancy to discuss what provisions she should make, in the event Tish and Marty couldn't get down to check on her.

'You're an authority on snow now, are you?' she snapped.

'Well, Mother, we do get quite a lot of it.'

She hated being called Mother. There was something so derogatory about the word.

'I've seen snow, Michael, and long before you ever did. What do you take me for, a Baluba?'

That got rid of him.

The snow melted, and with it all hopes of a white Christmas. Nancy could think of nothing worse. It would cause mayhem on the roads, and the council workers were never prepared with enough salt to grit beyond the main streets of the town. And Lord above, the panic buying, sliced pans flying off the shelves as if the country were on the brink of an apocalypse. No, no. A snow-free Christmas would suit Nancy just fine. She would pack her little suitcase and Marty would drive her up to Dublin, where she'd take a flight to London and spend a few days with Stella, to see what kind of situation she was after landing herself in this time.

Nancy had spent a great deal of time and money assembling a wardrobe that would divest her youngest child of the notion they were all peasants in Tramore. No synthetic fabrics, only silk or cotton blouses, her lambswool cardigan, and a cashmere scarf that she would throw casually over her shoulder, with its label facing out. Italian shoes and navy leather gloves. Her best foundation wear. Her toilet bag. When all of this was arranged in Nancy's suitcase, she took down the dust sleeve containing her Michael Kors handbag. With so many compartments, it really was the perfect bag for travelling. It had been a good investment.

She needed to fill her prescriptions at Dunford's and buy a few essentials before the flight. Pocket tissues. Silvermints. On her walk to the shops, Nancy passed the odd dirty splotch of snow. How fresh the air felt now. She drew it down into her lungs. At the brow of Gallwey's Hill a blast of sunlight momentarily blinded her, she squinted against it and began the descent into town. She could make out the figure of a man coming towards her. He was long-limbed and wiry, and as he came closer she could see that he was dressed in a military-style overcoat that flapped with his stride. His bootlaces were undone, and on his head he wore a deer-skin cap. His nose was Roman, and he'd a ring through one nostril. Instantly, she knew this was Ben Jacob.

'Hello,' he said.

By the time Nancy composed a response, he had passed.

That same afternoon, she was out the back empty-ing the kitchen bin into the grey wheelie bin, for fear it would stink up the kitchen while she was away. Some-thing caught her eye. A small projectile had landed on her lawn. It appeared to come from Vonnie's side of the privet hedge. Nancy dropped the pedal bin, and went down the garden to investigate. She was astounded to see a dozen, or more, hand-rolled cigarette butts scattered about the place. Having identified the most recent one, she picked it up for inspection. Nancy sniffed the charred stub, which confirmed to her that these weren't cigarettes at all, but marijuana joints. And the culprit was Ben Jacob.

Vonnie would have to be told. Peculiar as she was, under no circumstances would she tolerate drug use, or allow a neighbour's property to be used as an ashtray. They'd have to put the run on the nephew. Nancy knew his sort. She knew, the minute she laid eyes on him. He reminded her of the wasters Stella used to pal around with. She'd intended to call on Vonnie anyway, with a Christmas card and a poinsettia, before heading away to London.

After a brief and highly unsatisfactory exchange on Vonnie's porch, during which Vonnie revealed a spiteful streak that was nothing short of appalling, Nancy returned home with both the card and the plant.

Her humour was still venomous the next morning, when Marty drove her to Dublin to catch her flight. 'I don't want to go to England at all,' she told him. 'I've a mind to stay at home and spend Christmas with yourself and Tish.'

'I know,' said Marty. The Intercity bus in front of them was straddling two lanes.

'Vonnie's nephew,' Nancy went on, 'the one filming the goats – he's a druggie.'

'What?'

'He's a drug addict.'

'How do you know?'

'He's been throwing marijuana joints into my garden. I found them yesterday.'

'They're probably just roll-ups.'

'Why do you all treat me like a stupid old woman?'

Her voice cracked, next would come the tears. Two hours to Dublin. Marty apologized. He didn't mean anything by it. Nancy had the pocket tissues out.

'I called to give Vonnie her Christmas present,' she said. 'I tried to tell her, to warn her. And would you believe she hunted me? She closed the door in my face.' Mucus clogged Nancy's throat. She coughed and blew hard into a tissue. 'I think I'll go to the guards when I get home after Christmas.'

'Ah, now,' said Marty. 'I wouldn't do that. You'll be neighbours long after the nephew is gone.'

By St Stephen's Day, Nancy was ready to leave London. Stella's flat was a dump. It was in Brixton and the place was full of blacks, and if you said a word against them, Stella would come down on you like a ton of bricks. She'd a poster on the kitchen wall that said: 'No Irish. No Blacks. No Dogs.' As if there was any comparison. What was wrong with Stella? She'd put no effort into making the place look Christmassy. Not so much as a tree, and the only cards she had were the ones that Nancy and Tish had sent her. All the same, she'd the where-withal to roast a turkey crown and put a dinner together. It was grand, apart from the big show she made of setting fire to the Christmas pudding. There was an Englishness to this custom that Nancy found, frankly, quite offensive. But overall, things had been going fine until she mentioned Vonnie's nephew and the marijuana.

'You can't go to the guards,' Stella said.

'Why not?'

She rolled her eyes. 'It's only weed. Everybody smokes it. Even the guards.'

'They do not,' Nancy snapped. 'Neither do I, and I know for a fact your sister doesn't.'

'Maybe you should,' Stella said. 'Both of you.'

When she got home, Nancy didn't see, and tried not to think about, the people next door. She heard them coming and going at peculiar times of the day. The evidence of Ben Jacob's drug habit had been removed from the lawn. Nancy knew from local radio reports that the goat demonstrations were now a daily occurrence on the quay so she stayed away from Waterford. She avoided Café Caruso and the Prom too. Most days, she rarely went further than the shed, to fill a scuttle with coal and sticks. Once a week, she dropped a new ball of lard into the birdfeeder that hung from the apple tree. The garden was in a seasonal coma, the shrubs were brittle and burnt by frost, the metallic soil disturbed only by the claws of cats, looking for a place to shit. Whenever Nancy saw one squat and lift its tail she rapped loudly on the windowpane. She could hardly bear to look at the patio. Rainwater had pooled in the folds of the tarpaulin covering the garden furniture, she'd stuck a breeze block on top of it, in case it took flight in the wind and got entangled in one of the tall trees – or worse still, billowed over the privet into Vonnie's domain.

It was her birthday at the end of January. Tish brought her to a show at the Theatre Royal and afterwards to a tapas restaurant on Keizer Street, where she ordered a bottle of white wine and terracotta bowls of smoked almonds and green olives. The olives were stuffed with anchovy paste; Nancy spat them into her serviette for fear she would vomit on the spot.

'There's something I've been meaning to ask you,' Tish said.

Nancy braced herself.

'But I don't want you to get upset.'

'I'm all ears.'

'Have you fallen out with Vonnie?'

Nancy picked a bit of lint from her cardigan sleeve and dropped it on the floor.

'I'd rather keep myself to myself,' she said.

Tish phoned more often after that. But she always seemed to be on her way somewhere, with the mobile on speaker. Nancy couldn't hear her half the time, and she didn't always have the patience to listen closely or ask Tish to repeat what she had said, so she'd just hang up and pretend they were cut off. On bad days, she didn't answer her phone at all.

Spring arrived, without warning, one Sunday morning. Nancy'd been lying in, and when she got up to draw the curtains, she was dazzled by sunlight. It reached into every corner of the house, revealing cobwebs and dust balls that'd been gathering for months.

She made a cup of tea and took an old bath towel outside to wipe down the patio chairs. Later, she would get Marty to shift the breeze block and the tarpaulin. She'd do it herself, get rid of the damn things for once and for all, but it wasn't worth the risk of crushing her foot with the block. She sat on the patio and drank her tea. The garden was rousing at last. Ferns unfurled, and tiny white petals speckled the grass around the blackthorn, daffodils seemed to have shot up overnight beneath the apple trees, and all around the borders there were spurts of violet and coltsfoot. Nancy closed her eyes. Birds rustled in the ivy, she could hear something slow and heavy push through the undergrowth by the boundary wall. A badger, or possibly a fox. Something no worse than herself. She took the air and let the pale sun warm her pyjama legs. Kicking off her slippers, she wiggled her toes. What a shame it would be to waste such a morning. Moss had filled the gaps between the paving stones, there was lichen and liverwort too. But she'd tackle the moss first, she'd take a yard brush to it.

Nancy had scrubbed halfway down the garden path when Vonnie appeared above the privet. She was on a stepladder, her skinny arms snapping at the air with a garden shears.

'Hello, stranger!'

Nancy scrubbed harder and did not look up. It was too soon to be pruning the privet, it would grow unevenly if you went at it too early. Fresh clippings tumbled on to the grass on Nancy's side of the hedge.

'Ah, don't be cross with me,' said Vonnie, over the *snap-snap-snap* of her shears.

Nancy pushed harder on the spiky orange bristles, scrubbing faster. She was sweating now in her winter pyjamas. Her cheeks were burning and her hair was surely fierce. Vonnie's laughter tinkled like teaspoons on china. Still, Nancy would not look up. On and on she scrubbed, until she was within a few feet of the privet. She stopped suddenly then, and swung the yard brush over the top of the hedge. Vonnie ducked and swayed like a boxer. She seemed to lose her balance and the stepladder began to wobble. As it toppled, Vonnie let out a puny cry. Her eyes met Nancy's for the briefest moment before she disappeared.

There may have been a bit of a rattle and a soft thump, but once she was gone what Nancy noticed most was the stillness. Except for the faraway peal of the Holy Cross church bell, the garden was gloriously quiet.

Kamikaze

It was a Monday in July and Manhattan was sweltering. I needed to sit down, to cool down. I'd walked forty blocks only to find the Chelsea Hotel closed for renovations. Beneath a tower of scaffolding, a young fella with curls springing out from beneath his hard hat was flinging splintered sheets of MDF into a skip. 'Residents only,' he said. Then he turned his broad brown shoulder to me and got on with his work.

Grace had never heard of the Chelsea Hotel.

'What do you want to go there for?' she said.

To her mind it was high time I got a job. She'd one lined up for me and all, waitressing at some Irish bar in midtown called McCool's.

'Have you ever met anyone named McCool?' I said.

'Look it, Stella,' she said. 'Do you want the job or not?'

I told her I did, and she told me I was to start on the brunch shift that weekend. She showed me how to carry plates three and four at a time. I walked the length of our railroad apartment with Delft wobbling on my outstretched arms and her on at me to look where I was going and not at what I was doing. I'd be serving eggs Benedict and Florentine, or the full Irish if you wanted it: two rashers, two sausages, black and white pudding, eggs over easy, slithering around on the plate. There was a bottle of Chef sauce on every table. For fifteen dollars, you got coffee refills and a watery Bloody Mary. I'd make a hundred on a good day, Grace said.

'What's the big deal about this Chelsea Hotel?'

'The song, you know – Leonard Cohen?'

Grace curled her lip.

'Edith Piaf? Brendan Behan?'

She made her big fucken deal face, dropped her head between the fleshy white inside of her thighs, and continued to paint her toenails.

Grace had been in America a month by then, she was the one who'd set it up. One minute we were doing our finals in Cork, the next she was on a plane to New York and I was back in Tramore. My mother was mad to dispatch me to my brother Michael in Canada. He did his best to scupper her plan by assuring me there were jobs aplenty at the Peavey Mart in Moose Jaw for graduates with degrees in Art History. 'Look at her,' Mum would say to my sister Tish, 'four years down in Cork and what's she got to show for it?'

I thought I'd burst with gratitude the day Grace rang from New York, telling me to come on over. She'd found a sublet on the Lower East Side, a six-floor walk-up. Not a bother to her, she had agricultural stamina and a string of inter-county medals to prove it.

On the day I arrived, I cut the legs off my jeans and went to Best Buy for a thirty-dollar fan. My giblets were stewing, sweat bubbled in the hot creases where skin touched off skin, behind my knees, beneath my breasts. Though it hardly seemed possible, our apartment felt hotter than it was out on the street; Grace put her Converse on the fire escape and I did the same, then I traipsed around barefoot in her wake. We'd no shower, just an old enamel bathtub in the kitchen, it was covered by a wooden hatch that you lifted and hooked on to the wall whenever you needed it. I filled the bath with cold water, stripped to my bra and knickers and got in. We sat there, at opposite ends, Grace and me, drinking Snapple and listening to the Z train trundle across the river to Brooklyn.

Things grew awkward between us during those first few days beneath the hulk of the Williamsburg Bridge. Its concrete ramp ran parallel to our only window, more than once a driver caught me staring into the traffic and honked or waved back through the trusswork. Grace wanted to stick an air conditioner in the window, she said we could go halves once I got paid. Until then, she closed it for security, and I opened it again, in the hope of circulating some air. All it did was pump more heat and noise and fumes in on top of us. I liked to climb out the window in the early morning and sit on the fire escape, watching the Department of Sanitation collect sour-smelling garbage bags off the kerb.

I wasn't ready to sling hash at McCool's. I wanted to mosey around and take it all in. The boys outside the bodega on Clinton Street hissed when they saw me coming. On Houston, people milled about clutching beakers of iced coffee. Cargo-panted hipsters, dainty Asian women in black shift dresses, office workers with half-moons of sweat beneath their shirtsleeves. All of us on the hot nervy brink of eruption. Never before had I experienced such heat, it assaulted you from all angles: laundromats, pizzerias, hot-dog carts. Even the grates on the sidewalk exhaled gusts of torrid air. And I loved every bit of it. I loved the way the earth trembled whenever a train passed below. I loved the stampede rhythm of the carriages, the human swell that rolled up the subway steps and poured out on to the street. I loved the way people scarpered in every direction, and the way Fifth Avenue rolled out in a silver ribbon before me. For the first time in my life, I felt at home.

Ten miles a day I must have been walking. There wasn't a bother on me until the curly lad turned me away from the Chelsea Hotel. I felt suddenly exhausted. It was only a few blocks to Madison Square. I could have rested under the prow of the Flatiron and worked up a second wind. But with my genetic predisposition for stubbornness, or maybe pure stupidity, I limped on down the shady side of the street until, too tired to go on, I stalled outside a condemned-looking dive bar called Mikey's.

I pushed the door and it opened. The place was long and dark, it reeked of bleach and stagnant spillage. There were no customers, just a barmaid on Rollerblades. She was about my age, peroxide blonde and dressed in a scrap of denim. Her bare shoulders were tattooed with angel wings. I sat unnoticed at the bar while she hummed along to the jukebox and glided around, shuffling her deck of beer mats and dealing them out in hands of five on to the red Formica tabletops. When she reached the back room, she pirouetted through a set of saloon doors and vanished into the Ladies.

I moved to the other end of the bar, where I could not be ignored. All that separated me from the toilets was a pool table which, I noticed, had at either end a cube of blue chalk dangling by a chain. In a display cabinet on the wall, four long leather pouches hung like animal carcasses, each branded with a name in gold-leaf italics.

– *Barry*
– *Buddy*
– *Ed*
– *Marlene*

The saloon doors swung open and Blondie reappeared.

'You here about the *jawb*?' She spun around to face me and rolled backwards, as if on casters, in behind the bar. With one hand, she reached inside the fridge, and with the other she picked up a cordless phone, into which I heard her yodel, 'Someone's here about the *jawb*.'

She planted a bottle of Budweiser on the bar and told me 'Clancy' wouldn't be long. I slugged it down to the ankles and was about to ask for another when a trapdoor flew open and out of the ground crawled a hairy, red-faced ogre, in a Grateful Dead T-shirt and filthy blue jeans. This, I reckoned, was the eponymous 'Mikey', aka Clancy. He barrelled down the bar in my direction, his eyes sucking me in. I knew the look well enough. He was trying to reconstruct the whys and wherefores of me being there. Where had he been drinking when he met me? Mikey Clancy would never have offered me a job sober. That much was obvious.

'How's it goin'?' I said.

'Irish,' he muttered, as if it explained a lot.

He grabbed a can of Pabst Blue Ribbon from the fridge and downed it with hostile thirst. He told me this was no Irish bar and he didn't give a wrinkled rat's ass if I knew how to pull a pint. Shelley – he butted his head in Blondie's direction – was moving to weekends, and if I wanted to cover midweek I'd better know how to tend 'an American bar'.

I was quizzed on country music and the constituents of a Long Island iced tea. I must have given a better than expected account of myself, because Clancy's features softened. Merely ugly now, he no longer looked like an argument waiting to happen. He pulled a roll of banknotes out from under his pink marbled belly, peeled off a twenty and told me to buy a *Bartender's Bible*. I could feel him take the measure of me as I walked towards the door.

The next day, I went to Barnes & Noble on Astor Place, shoplifted a cocktail book and read it on the grass in Washington Square Park before setting off for Mikey's. I was wearing flip-flops, my denim cut-offs and a black lacy Penneys vest that, judging by the putrid look Grace shot me, might have been underwear. Clancy didn't comment except to say that redheads made more money with their hair down. He put a float in the register and told me to give a free Kamikaze shot – a buyback – for every fourth drink. Have one yourself, he said, and if you don't want one, fake it. Cocktails were five bucks at Happy Hour. I was to use speed-rack liquor only.

'Got that, Irish?'

'Got it.'

'Sweet.'

Away he squelched. And I pulled the scrunchie out of my hair.

I had exactly five customers on my first shift at Mikey's. A morose bag of bones arrived bang on Happy Hour, drank a couple of dirty gin martinis and was on his way out when three preppy lads hopped on to the barstools opposite me. They ordered a round of Black and Tans and ogled the bras that hung above the top shelf like bunting, encouraged by the ceiling fans to occasionally flutter. 'It's more fun here on the weekends,' said one. They hooked it then, leaving three beer-soaked dollars on the bar. I took a pickled egg from the Mason jar beside the register and I watched myself eat it in the mirror, while some hick on the jukebox warbled about bourbon and heartache.

Hours passed before the door creaked open again,

and in lurched a long-legged yoke, who'd the look of
fifty but could've been a derelict forty-two. His name
was Tim – information imparted in a manner that
suggested he was a regular. He downed a pint of
Guinness and, through a slit in his cream-soaked
whiskers, asked for another. When I went to put his
pint on the bar he reached out awkwardly to take it
from my hand and the head slopped over the lip of
the glass. Stout dribbled down his fingers. He sighed
emphatically at the mess, or maybe at the inconveni-
ence of it. Then, lifting one buttock off the stool, he
reached into his trouser pocket and produced a hanky
the size of a tea towel. He wiped the slop away and
asked me where I was from.

'Ireland.'

Next thing, his wallet was out, flopped open in the
palm of his hand and presented to me in the way a
butcher might show you a steak.

'My ex was Irish.'

He tapped his finger on a photo of a woman with a
voluminous perm.

'She's pretty,' I lied.

He ignored me and asked where Shelley was.

'Moved to weekends.'

'She's a dancer.'

'Your ex?'

'No. Shelley.'

Tim bought me a beer and our conversation spluttered on for the guts of two hours. He pointed a dirty
finger at the bras above the top shelf, and told me they

belonged to the weekend bartenders. 'The bigger the bra, the faker the tits.' He took a gulp of stout and leered at me over the rim of the glass. 'Yours are too small, they gotta be real.'

I pretended not to hear and ate another pickled egg. When I'd finished, he claimed to have seen Clancy pissing in the Mason jar. I slid a Kamikaze down the bar and called last orders.

The roll and clank of Mikey's shutters announced to the neighbourhood that I was locking up. Abandoned as the street appeared, I knew it wasn't possible to be alone in Manhattan, even in the Meatpacking District, which, according to Grace, was populated by rodents and crack whores exclusively. There was a TV on the neighbour's stoop, a black hole where the screen used to be, as though somebody had put a boot through it. The sidewalk was empty except for the stubby fire hydrants that stood like sentinels at opposite ends of the street. Making a beeline for Eighth Avenue, I was relieved to see a cab come towards me with its roof-light on. It slid along the kerb and stopped. I hopped in and, comforted by the click of the door locks, spread myself across the cool leatherette of the back seat.

We'd gone a few blocks before I caught the cab driver's eyes in the mirror; they were bloodshot, with dark, wiry brows. He disengaged the meter. The moment of recognition moved like a blade across my tongue. It was him – Tim. He had trapped me. I tried to shout, to scream, but nothing came out. He drove in silence. All I could do was watch the numbered streets descend, down, down, down, through Greenwich Village and into SoHo. Was this it? The end of the road? I wondered how my life might have turned out in Moose Jaw and I imagined my mother (even in grief) saying I'd always gone too far, how she knew I would come to a bad end. She'd probably go on about the time we saw a child being pulled from the sea. A black-haired boy in luminous green trunks. And the way I wouldn't stop crying about him. Didn't I realize he'd ruined everybody's life, especially his poor mother's? She was blue in the face from telling me what happens to children who go out too far. 'They drown, Stella! They drown!' Through the cab window, Manhattan flashed by me in technicolour bursts of neon. Nail parlours, diners and drugstores. Corner delis that never closed and, in their windows, flags that I did not recognize. So many countries I would not live to see.

I didn't notice the guy we hit until he was thrown on to the bonnet and bounced off the windscreen. You'd have expected a bigger thud, really. He could have been a cat or a seagull, for all the noise he made.

Tim slammed on the brakes and my forehead smacked into the perspex screen that separated us. He jumped out of the cab. I tried to open my door but it was locked.

We were somewhere in Chinatown, people had

begun to gather around, talking excitedly in what I supposed was Mandarin, though it could have been Korean. A teenager in a bone-white shirt and sky-blue baggies was lying on the road, he looked like a kitchen porter from one of the noodle houses. He was probably taking out the garbage when we hit him. Now, he was thrashing around in the gutter, clutching his side.

There was a police siren and flashing red and white lights. A voice boomed through a loudhailer that nobody was to move the casualty. Next thing, a lady cop opened the cab door and motioned for me to get out. Her lips were brown and shiny, and her eyelashes were long as spider legs. She was talking to me, but I couldn't make the words out. My head hurt, I touched it gently, and when I took my hand away, my fingers were covered in blood.

'Do you understand what I am saying?'

I held out my hand to show her the blood.

'Do you speak English?'

'I'm Irish.'

'You're injured, miss. Stay where you are.'

The lady cop went back to the squad car that was parked, lopsided, on the kerb with its lights still flashing.

While she was distracted, I noticed a gap in the crowd and slipped away through it. One of my flip-flops had gone missing in the crash. I kicked the other one off. When I got to the next junction and saw a sign saying Grand Street, I started to run. All I had to do was make it to the bridge and then I was safe.

Nobody would know I was illegal. Nobody would send me back to Tramore.

Grace was stretched out on the futon, eating a quart of Chunky Monkey and listening to her favourite Cranberries CD. She shot up when she saw me, and the ice cream carton rolled on to the floor.

'Jesus Christ, Stella!' she said.

'I'm fine.'

'Were you raped?'

'No.'

'What happened?'

'Nothing. I'm going to bed.'

'But you're bleeding,' she said.

'Would you just fucking drop it? I told you I was fine.'

It was true. I did turn out fine. What became of Grace, I couldn't tell you.

Love Comes Late Around Here

Ted Burke, the butcher, awoke at half past seven. It was March, and the sky beyond his bedroom window was obsidian. He thumbed the wheel of his clock radio on, fell back on the pillows and, closing his eyes, he listened to the London Philharmonic perform *Madama Butterfly*. One of his favourites, Dame Kiri Te Kanawa singing '*Un bel dì, vedremo*'. So powerful and refined, he'd never seen or heard such a woman in real life. Supposing she stepped out of the clock radio now and stood there at the foot of the bed in her fine opera gown and jewels. Supposing she pinned him to the mattress with her proud brown eyes and murmured, 'How did you sleep, Thaddeus?' What choice would he have but to cower beneath the bedspread and pray. One fine day, indeed.

Not ideal, this business of having to shave in the dark. The soft amber bulb of the bathroom cabinet was too imprecise, but you couldn't waste an entire morning waiting for daylight. Ted did the best he could under the circumstances and nicked himself twice. There was too much blood in him, it took five scraps of toilet paper to stop it dripping into his breakfast. Two poached eggs, one slice of soda bread with a scrape of butter. No salt. Doctor's orders. The clock above the Aga was running slow. It would persist withholding the correct time from him until he changed the battery. In the meantime, he supposed the kitchen wireless would have to do. *Pip-pip-pip*, it went, to signal the eight o'clock news.

He sank his dentures into the bread. A Latvian woman in her thirties had been murdered in Mullingar. A man, who was known to the victim, was helping Gardaí with their inquiries. No doubt he is, the cur. You'd have to wonder about these Eastern Europeans, they were a rough bunch. The men, especially, had a brutish disregard for human life. If you were to ask Ted Burke, it was a communist trait and not at all in keeping with the Irish way. Only, he would rather not be quizzed on such matters.

Through the window, the sky above Tramore Bay was spacious, with hopeful darts of silvery blue. There would be no sea fog today, thank God. January and most of February had been mired in the cursed vapour. It had a way of sucking the joy out of you. Today, he'd put on his mackintosh and flat cap, he'd deliver the breakfast meats to Muriel Power's guest house, then he'd keep going and take a stroll down the Promenade. Should the stars align, as he ardently hoped they would, he might cross paths with Vonnie Jacob. Such serendipity would be slow to come around again. An encounter would surely be a sign. Yes, if he met her, he would somehow find the courage to ask her out.

The prospect of revealing his intentions put a

tangle in his gut; it wasn't unlike the feeling he had the first time she came into his shop, all smiles and chat, as if they were old friends newly reacquainted. They had not met before, of that he was quite certain. Vonnie Jacob was not a woman you'd easily forget. What did she want? A chicken. Free range and organic. He shook his head. He'd need notice to procure such a thing. Her eyes were turquoise and merry. Ah, she said, lowering her head to peer through the glass at the trays of liver and tripe. He contemplated the glamorous roll of her hair and wished to Christ he'd something other than entrails to offer. She rested her fingers on the glass countertop, the nails were pale as clamshells, and in place of a wedding band she wore a man's signet ring.

Oxtail! she declared. I'll take four of those. Ted plunged his hand into the meat and dug out the thicker cuts. I can have the chicken in tomorrow, he said. She replied that Friday would be fine, and took her bag of oxtails off the counter. A most unusual-looking woman. She was, he supposed, a visitor, but to ask her business would be brazen. Unzipping the purse she held in her hand, she asked how much she owed him. Friday, he replied. You can settle with me when you come for the chicken. She smiled. All her own teeth, small and white and slightly crooked around the incisors. I'm Vonnie Jacob, she said. He whipped the blood-streaked polythene glove off and extended his hand to meet hers. Thaddeus Burke. She smiled again. I know, she said. Isn't it written above the door?

He'd thought long and hard about the matter, talking himself into and out of asking her to accompany him to the Theatre Royal. He was as ready now as he would ever be. The only thing he felt sure of was that the invitation should not be made on the butcher shop floor. Pulling the flat cap down over his ears, he set off down Pond Road towards the town. Work was progressing on the Japanese Gardens, the community enterprise lads were hard at it in their hi-visibility vests, clearing ditches and hammering lengths of wood together for fencing and, Ted supposed, for gazebos, bridges and what have you. They'd all sorts of dignitaries lined up for the ribbon cutting. Japanese descendants of Lafcadio Hearn. To his shame, Ted hadn't heard of the man until he read about the building works in *The Munster Express*. Soon the place would be exploding with blossom trees, their perfume drifting across the top town. He imagined Vonnie Jacob strolling through the gardens, white petals falling at her feet.

Already the roads were busy; lights on full beam swung around corners, tyres splattered puddle water about the place. Through the windscreens, drivers slugged from travel mugs, more focused on their children in the seats behind them than on the cars ahead of them. Why didn't children walk to school any more? He couldn't see any justification for this daily cortège of SUVs through the town, raising dirt that clung to the shopfronts and windows, polluting the air with their exhausts. He hated the *parp-parping* of car horns at the school gate. The only thing this so-called 'school run' was good for was encouraging laziness in children. There was a time when it was unusual to see a fat, or even a chubby, boy – a time when heft in a child was a medical condition, and not a consequence of indolence. It was true that he was getting crabbier by the day. It was the word his daughters used when they were sick of listening to him. 'Don't be so *crabby*, Daddy.' Their time would come too. He was only sorry he wouldn't be around to see it and say to them: see now, what did I tell you?

The keyhole in the shop door was stiff with sea salt again. A squirt of WD-40 would do the trick. He left the cages over the windows and slipped inside to package up the sausages and pudding for Muriel. Eleven would be time enough to open today. If a single customer came before the Angelus at noon, he'd be amazed. That was the way since the supermarkets had opened. Three of them, now. But he wouldn't be hounded out of business, he would dig his heels in, sandwiched between the Vape shop and the bookies. Thaddeus Burke, family butcher, would leave Patrick Street in a box.

In the Stella Maris guest house, there was nowhere to put down the breakfast meats. Every surface in the kitchen was clouded with scouring cream. Muriel Power, slicing a tea brack on an ironing board, had a foot-long knife in her hand. The blade on it was ferocious.

'Will you take a bit with butter, Ted?'

93

Although pleased to be asked, he said he wouldn't trouble her. And Muriel, relieved that he'd the manners to decline, said she wouldn't force it on him.

She brought the knife down again. 'Such a commotion this morning.'

'Was there?' said Ted.

'Guards, ambulance, the whole shebang. Did you not hear it?'

'No.'

'Beyond the Doneraile?'

He shook his head.

Muriel seemed disappointed. 'Right,' she said. 'Leave the bag on the floor and I'll get your money from the cashbox.'

'You're grand,' said Ted, backing out the door from the chemical stench. 'I'll be up this way in an hour, and you can settle with me then.' He was a vinegar man himself. White in gallon drums, it was cheaper and safer than sprays or foams. But Muriel, she was mad for ammonia.

Her ginger cat was curling around the door frame as he was leaving, and didn't he flatten its tail with the heel of his shoe. The cat hissed at him and shot under an armchair.

Muriel flashed the blade. 'That boyo is highly strung.' She lowered it again, to finish her job on the brack.

He made his way through the garden that led to the coal runner's lane, and beyond it the brow of Train Hill. There was a time when girls stood at the bottom to squeal and cheer as lads, competing for their approval, raced each other to the top. It had been years since he'd climbed the hill – and the last time, he considered himself lucky to reach the summit alive. Now, he was in such a condition he'd to be mindful on the descent. A patch of black ice or engine grease could send him tumbling, roly-poly, down on to the Lower Branch Road. If the fall didn't kill him, the humiliation surely would.

At the foot of the hill he spied Midge Maguire smoking outside The Kiosk. She saw him too, dropped her cigarette and stamped on it. Such an awful woman, even cancer wouldn't take her. As Ted passed the closed amusement arcades he noticed the footpath was pocked with grey welts of chewing gum. At the end of the strip there was a man standing on a balcony in one of the holiday apartments. His dressing gown flapped open in the breeze, revealing white underpants and an impressive hairy chest. He was shouting into a mobile phone and taking gulps from a green and gold can. Ted quickened his pace on the pavement below.

Blast it, but weren't the storm drains blocked again. Strand Road was flooded. He'd have to go back past the hairy muscleman to find a dry route on to the Gentleman's Slip. It was, by his estimation, the best vantage point for spotting Vonnie on her daily walk. Supposing she accepted his invitation, supposing they made a regular habit of going out. What would his daughters say? They had great sport at the Christmas dinner table proposing lady friends for him. Tramore was bursting at the seams with widows, they said. And spinsters too. Wasn't Muriel Power saving herself for him? The younger one suggested internet dating, setting the older one off on a fit of shrieking. Their husbands sat mute, paper crowns on their heads. His grandson, Shane, muttered 'for fuck's sake' and went back to swiping the screen on his new smartphone. They were a right pair, his daughters, when you put them together. All it took was a bottle of wine to discharge the wickedness in them. He did not think he would introduce them to Vonnie. They wouldn't know what to make of her. They would think she was a hippie, and that he had lost the run of himself.

The stone bench on the slip was slick with sea spray, there was nothing for it but to walk the strand, like a man hoping to find something he had lost. People came to the beach with their kites and their children and their surfboards. The ones who had no purpose for being there parked on the Prom and stared miserably at the horizon through their windscreens. Did he really need a reason to be there? Wasn't walking on the beach a purpose in itself? Up ahead of him a young woman with a dog was swinging a stick above her head, launching tennis balls into the sky. Sometimes the dog leapt up and, in a sinewy twist, caught the ball mid-air, other times it missed and went bounding down the beach, following the ball's arc, and returning with it in his maw. Ted watched their inky silhouettes and he envied them. Maybe he'd get himself a dog, after all, for the company. It would get him out of the house. A little terrier with a taste for scraps. Not a bad calling, to be a butcher's dog.

Beyond the embankment, the beachfront cafés were getting ready to open. At Caruso's, Oliver Forte was putting out tables for the smokers and the dog walkers. He was Ted Burke's best customer. They shared a love of musical theatre and quality beef. Both men were sticklers for traceability. A slaughterhouse in Tipperary delivered an E-grade carcass that Ted butchered with great care especially for Oliver, who came every Thursday afternoon on his mint-green moped to collect two dozen steaks for his weekend diners. He'd inherited his uncle's fish 'n' chip shop and, rather than sell it on – as the locals thought he might – didn't he move down from Belfast and transform Forte's into a proper restaurant that he renamed after the great Italian tenor. Caruso's sold imported olive oil and coffee beans, and during the summer months he'd a cart selling tutti-frutti- and amaretto-flavoured ice cream on the Prom. Such a way he had with the ladies. Older women, in particular, were mad about him. Ted had seen them, the coquettish ones nibbling on the little biscuits he'd rest on the lip of their saucers, and the loud ones, all hands and capped teeth, cackling about what a terrible man he was. Just terrible!

Oliver Forte was nobody's fool. What he was, however, was a homosexual. Ted hadn't known many homosexuals in his time, but anyone with an eye in his head could see that Oliver was one. Watching him now, standing outside the restaurant, barrel chest to the breeze, looping an apron over his head and tying it behind, Ted decided that if Vonnie declined to join him at the Theatre Royal, he would give the tickets to Oliver Forte instead, as a thank you for his custom.

A *split-splat* on his cap. He took it off to make sure it was rain and not bird droppings. The weather was on the turn, he could feel it. I'm a woman for all seasons, Vonnie once told him. It was during the last hurricane, when anyone with a whit of sense stayed indoors. She landed in the shop, wild-eyed and windswept, inquiring if he'd such a thing as a rabbit loin. He didn't, but he knew where to get one: from the same organic butcher in Waterford where he bought her Friday chicken, which he stripped of its shrink-wrap and decorated with rosemary sprigs, before presenting it to her as his own, for three euros less than he'd paid for it.

The sea drizzle had him chilled to the bone. The invitation would have to wait for another day. He'd warm up with a mug of tea when he got back to the shop. What difference, he supposed, if he made the invitation there. She'd be in on Friday for her chicken and he'd ask her then, casually, as though it had just occurred to him. She could let him down lightly.

On the Branch Road, he saw a hearse approaching and stopped for a moment to take off his cap and let it pass. Ted blessed himself, and the hearse driver nodded. Old age was cruel and loneliness a bastard. Was he after losing the run of his wits entirely? Traipsing around the town like a pervert, waiting to ambush a woman on her morning walk. How foolish he'd been to make such a song and dance about it. He felt relieved, now, that he hadn't bumped into Vonnie, after all.

Muriel opened her front door before he'd time to ring the bell. 'Shocking news,' she gasped, waving a twenty-euro note at him. 'That carry-on beyond the Doneraile.'

'What carry-on?'

'The woman who bought Tom Ryan's house – do you know who I mean?'

'No. I don't think I do.' The rain was coming down heavy now.

'I'd say she was of the other persuasion.'

Ted pulled his collar up around his ears.

'Well,' said Muriel. 'The postman found her dead in the garden.'

'Good God.'

'Midge Maguire called in to tell me. The poor woman was soaked – apparently, she'd been there for days.'

'Now that you mention it,' said Ted. 'There was a hearse . . .'

Muriel blessed herself with the twenty-euro note. He wanted to snatch the money but her grip on it was hermetic.

'Did you ever meet her?'

'Who?'

She eyeballed him. 'The woman who bought Tom Ryan's house.'

'I don't think so.'

A puddle had formed around his feet, his socks were getting wet.

'There but for the grace of God,' said Muriel.

She held out the money and he took it.

Sit, Lie, Stay

Marty Devine did not want to see his wife. He stood at the kitchen sink with his ear cocked and monitored her flat-footed progress. Tish was still upstairs, plodding across the bedroom carpet. The door to the en-suite closed and a fart ricocheted around the toilet bowl. His getaway would have to be quick. He took Buddy's lead from a coat hook in the hall and checked his pockets to make sure nothing was forgotten: wallet, phone, keys. Marty stepped outside and closed the door. He was reversing down the driveway by the time Tish appeared at the window in her dressing gown. She waved at him. He decided not to see her as he steered the Megane between the gateposts. You'd to be careful with a dog in the car.

On the coast road, there was the suggestion of a scorcher about the day. Little balls of white cloud skipped across the sky. As he rounded the cliff top, Marty looked out at the sea; it glistened like fish scales, a shoal of silver mackerel about to roll on to the shore. Buddy was expecting a walk, and when they passed the turn-off for the beach, the dog began to whine. He didn't stop until they pulled into the Maxol at the far end of town.

The young one behind the counter had feline yellow

eyes and cheekbones like razor blades. The name badge above her breast said *Evinka*. So this was what he'd been missing since he lost his job and Tish commandeered the car for work – another reason to feel bereft, this Slavic goddess. She turned to take his Marlboros from the metal trough of the tobacco machine, and a golden ponytail swished over her shoulder.

'Any fuel?'

'No.'

He scanned the chewing gum and chocolate bars for a reason to continue the conversation. Evinka didn't seem to mind. He picked up a Twix and placed it on the counter.

'Two for two euro,' she said.

He took another, and asked for a cigarette lighter.

'What colour?'

'Red,' Marty replied.

She pushed down on the button and a weak blue flame rose up out of it.

'Twelve-euro-fifty-cent.'

Walking across the forecourt, he noticed a lightness to his step. It felt like an old acquaintance, a skin you'd have a pint with if you ran into him. How long had it been since he'd gone out for a pint? Ages. He might go for one later. The thought was suddenly extinguished and the want gone off him when he caught sight of Buddy in the car, his black woolly head bobbing between the headrests, and the tongue hanging out the side of his mouth like a half-eaten slice of ham.

The child the dog had bitten was a friend of Evie, his daughter. Her name was Lucy and she wore gold sequinned runners and a matching JoJo bow on top of her head. Her hair was synthetic yellow like a doll's, and very, very long. She was a pretty child, if you ignored the flap of bloody skin hanging from her cheek where Buddy had taken a lump out of her.

Marty eyed the dog. 'You're one stupid fucker.'

The girls had been giving him a makeover in the back garden. They brushed him. They clipped sparkly hairslides to his coat. Tish took photos of them hugging the dog, put them on Facebook, and went inside to get a treat for Buddy. She returned with a bag of dried Bavarian pigs' ears. Lucy was dancing around, holding one on either side of her head, when the dog jumped up and bit her on the face. Marty heard the screaming. He ran outside to find Tish standing on the patio with her mouth open. Evie was running up and down the garden, flapping her hands, and squawking, 'Oh my God! Oh my God!' Buddy had fled the scene with the two pigs' ears. Lucy, poor thing, was in shock. Blood dripped like rubies from her cheek on to her feet. The golden shoes were ruined.

Mulcahy the vet was on the ring road, in one of those retail parks that has an acre of tarmac out the front. He was cute enough, he'd set up beside The Pet Barn, so there wasn't a dog owner from here to Carrick who didn't know where to find him. Apparently, he was now qualified to operate on exotic animals and all:

lizards, terrapins and – would you believe? – snakes. Marty heard this from Evie, who'd heard it from a boy in school, whose cousin kept a corn snake that got run over by a skateboard. The snake's name was Dollar Bill and Mulcahy had stitched him back together.

'He did in his eye.'

'He did so,' said Evie. 'Why do you never believe anything I say?'

Oscar Mulcahy, reptilian as he was, couldn't tell one end of a snake from the other. You could put your house on it.

It was just gone eight and nothing was open yet in the retail park. A battered Honda Civic pulled into a space opposite him, two stringy lads got out of it and drifted across the car park, they punched a code into a keypad on The Pet Barn wall. A moment later, the metal door swung open and they disappeared inside. Marty wondered if he told them the story, would they refund the twenty-kilo bag of Supadog that was slumped, unopened, against the utility room wall. Then again, he could give it to one of the dog owners he knew. The 'pet parents', Tish called them – usually when he'd taken longer than was necessary to walk Buddy. He'd be hanging up his North Face in the hall and she'd call out from the kitchen.

'How are the pet parents?'

He longed to shout back that she could do with a walk herself, that it might shift some of the lard off her arse.

Sooner or later, he'd have to tell the other dog

owners where Buddy had gone and what he'd done. Some would sympathize, others would silently judge him. Marty imagined the pinched face on Avril Stephens, pontificating about how you could keep dogs *or* children, not both. 'Never trust a mongrel,' she'd say, a troika of fanatically groomed Pomeranians prancing around her ankles. She already had the hump with him for not spilling the beans about 'that woman', who died in the house next door to Nancy. He wasn't going to please her with the details of Buddy's misdemeanour.

Through a windscreen smudged with midge corpses, Marty contemplated the infinite ugliness of his surroundings. He was corralled in a valley of concrete and glass. Beyond the flat-roofed warehouses and superstores lay two miles of dual carriageway, interrupted every couple of hundred yards by a roundabout that spun off into another retail or business park. A peloton was circling the Ballygunner roundabout; he could make out the livid red strip of the local cycling club. They were like fire ants, the sunshine bouncing off the carapace of their helmets. Traffic was unusually light. The heatwave had half the country on work to rule, from what Marty could make out.

He lit a cigarette and flicked the radio on. Maggie Crowe, the breakfast show presenter, was talking to the weatherman. She wanted to know if he was in favour of a hose pipe ban, given the threat of drought.

'It's a meteorologist's job to report the weather, not to remedy it,' he sniped.

'Do you have to be such a bollix about it?' said Marty.

'That's a matter for the local authority,' the meteorologist continued.

'We'll leave it there so,' Maggie said, cool as you like. She reminded her listeners that temperatures would 'soar to a record-breaking twenty-eight degrees in the sunny South-East today'.

Marty liked the cut of her jib. She'd a bedroom voice and a tendency towards breathlessness. You could imagine her whispering obscenities as she nuzzled on your earlobe. He'd seen pictures of Maggie Crowe on billboards along the roadside: 'Rise and Shine with the Early Bird' they said. And there she was, all fourteen stone and fifty-odd years of her, poured into a fun-run T-shirt. She looked like the sort of woman who'd be dynamite at selling raffle tickets. On the radio, she was filthy.

Lucy had been transferred to a hospital up in Dublin. She didn't need a skin graft, as it happened, just some dainty needlework by a nurse in 'plastics'.

'They could sue us,' Tish said, opening a second bottle of wine. 'And I wouldn't blame them if they did.'

At her insistence, Buddy was tied up outside, howling into the darkness. Marty was sat on a chair in the corner. He would've gladly swapped places with the dog.

'The scarring could be minimal,' he said.

She glowered at him over her wine glass.

'Don't. Just fucken don't. You do realize that Evie will never get another play date?'

He'd been collecting their daughter from the school gate since he'd been made redundant, and Tish had gone back to work full-time. It'd been over a year, and in that time he hadn't managed to negotiate a single play date. In the end, Tish stepped in and organized one. When the day finally came, herself and Evie were baking rocky road to beat the band. At one point, Marty strayed into the kitchen, opened the fridge, and found it crammed with two-litre bottles of minerals, as though they were expecting a dozen children, instead of just the one. That's how big a deal this feckin play date had become.

'We'll be like lepers when this gets out,' Tish sniffled. 'The only thing worse would be if you were a paedophile.'

'Would you calm the fuck down?'

'I'm not waiting for the guards to show up at the door, Martin. I want this settled, here and now.'

'Evie doesn't want the dog put down.'

'Evie's a child! You're an adult! Stop acting like a pet parent. Be a real parent. For once!'

His tea had gone cold. He got up and threw it down the sink, but as he turned to leave, Tish blocked the door and squared up to him. 'Do I have to bring the dog down to Mulcahy myself?' she said.

He arrived at Mulcahy's door at the same time as Burke the butcher. The old man nodded at Marty, and Marty nodded back, stepping aside to let him into the waiting room first. The butcher's dog, a fat Jack

Russell, toddled over and back from the chairs to the counter, its nails clacking like rat claws off the floor while Buddy lay on the cool tiles watching him.

The receptionist was on the phone. Marty sat down and, for want of something to do, he pulled out his mobile. Two missed calls and a text from Tish. He'd opened the text before it occurred to him to ignore it.

– *Milk and bread*

Marty stared at the phone. He imagined dropping it on the floor, stamping his foot as hard as he could on the screen, smashing it. The young one on reception had finished her call. One of the Phelan twins. She smiled at him. He got up and walked towards the counter. What was her name again? Ciara, was it? Or Sinéad? They were almost identical. He'd coached them in athletics, back in the day. One had taken bronze in the provincial cross-country. He didn't think it was this one.

The Phelan girl tapped his name and address into her computer. 'I'm floundered with the heat,' she said.

'All the same,' said Marty, 'we'll be sorry when it's gone.'

She peeked over the counter at Buddy. 'I'd say he's bet with that big coat on him.'

Marty looked from the dog to the girl and back at the dog again.

'And it's just a booster you're in for, is it?'

Buddy's tail walloped the floor. *Thwack, thwack, thwack.*

The mobile phone began to vibrate in his shirt

pocket. That was the thing about Tish, she'd the persistence of a bluebottle. It was the reason he'd married her.

'Back in a minute,' he said to the Phelan girl.

The automatic doors of The Pet Barn slid open and in Marty shot, straight down the canine accessories aisle, pulling Buddy in his wake. Caught by the scruff, the dog shook and butted his head in pointless revolt. Marty slapped his snout and rammed it into a black rubber muzzle. He tied the strap extra tight. Buddy cowered and tucked his tail between his legs. He began to whimper.

Over by the sacks of pet food, a woman with a price gun stopped what she was doing and glared at Marty as he dragged the dog towards the cashier.

Mizaru

Lorcan's back is long and his shoulders are broad. His shirt, the colour of ancient tree bark, is made of fine corduroy that stretches pleasingly over his scapulae. He's at the sink, peeling vegetables, mucky carrots with feathery stalks and parsnips that are covered in welts. They cost him a couple of euro at the farmers' market down the town. 'Too ugly for the super-market,' he'd said to the girls, 'but just wait until you taste them.'

Over his shoulder, Joanne looks out the window at the low white ripples of the sea entering the bay. The girls are lying on the bunk beds in their room. Ella, exhausted after surf camp, is sleeping. Marianne is reading, forever reading, novels about runaways with unresolved endings. Joanne worries about this as Lorcan scrapes the blade against the vegetables. The plughole gurgles with skin and mud, and on the wall the china clock is running twelve minutes slow. Joanne has resisted the urge to correct it. It's almost five o'clock on a Thursday in July. It may, in fact, be Wednesday. She cannot say for sure. They are on holidays.

Lorcan's hair curls like a toddler's at the nape of his neck and rests on his shirt collar. It has started to turn grey. An attractive shade of gunmetal, is how Joanne would describe the colour. She thinks about the soft black hair that covers his stomach and the small of his back. It's on his forearms too, stopping where his sleeves begin. He wears a leather band on his right wrist. Lorcan is a *ciotóg*, and she thinks this is what makes him so good with his hands.

He has chopped up all the carrots and parsnips, and uses the knife to slide them from the wooden board into a saucepan. They land with a clonk and he fills the pot with water, then, turning around to put it on the stovetop, he catches her eye.

'I know *you*,' he says

It makes her smile.

'Are the girls occupied?'

'More or less.'

Joanne turns the key in the bedroom door. He is already under the duvet, one arm behind his head. Her eyes follow the line of his other arm down to where his hand is working on his erection. She pulls her jeans and knickers off in one go and climbs on top of him. She fucks him and he clamps his hand over her mouth so the girls don't hear her whimper when she comes. Afterwards, she lies there listening to his heart thrum inside his chest. Lorcan is all vitality: sweat and semen, and she is intoxicated by the smell of him. Sometimes when they have sex the thought of how much she loves him makes her cry.

In the evening, they sit in the garden. The lawn slopes down to a stone wall and a gate that opens on to the cliff walk. The rickety picnic table sways beneath them as they eat; Joanne has put beach towels over the benches so the girls don't get splinters in their behinds. Lorcan has picked up a bag of charcoal for the barbecue, it sits on a jittery tripod, but does the job. He cooks chicken wings and corn cobs for the girls. After they've eaten, he throws on a couple of rib-eye steaks that hiss and spit and fill the air with the delicious smell of charred beef. Joanne drinks Rioja from a whiskey glass and watches her daughters doing cartwheels up and down the lawn. Their hair has been bleached by the sun, their legs are brown and lean. Though she is younger, Ella, the more gymnastic of the two, is showing Marianne how to do a walking crab.

Lorcan puts a dish of buttered carrots and parsnips on the picnic table and asks Joanne what she's thinking about.

'Just, that it's true,' she says, 'there really is nowhere nicer than Ireland.'

'If you get the weather.'

'If you get the weather,' Joanne agrees, and she pours him a glass of wine.

The girls carry the dirty plates into the house and return with four raspberry ripple wafers on the chopping board that Lorcan was using earlier. The ice cream tastes of garlic, but they eat it anyway. Above them the sky is hot pink, and half a mile beneath them the Promenade looks busy. Joanne is amazed at how far the music in the amusement park can travel, a throbbing bassline, punctuated by childish squeals from the fastest rides. The harder she listens, the louder it gets. Lorcan has promised the girls a go on the waltzer. Joanne will not go on any amusements; she watches the lights on the Ferris wheel rotate, and that alone is enough to turn her stomach.

'Big day tomorrow, ladies,' Lorcan says.

He whooshes the girls up the steps and leaves Joanne to tidy away the beach towels and the wine glasses. He has booked bicycles for them to ride along the Greenway, a disused railway line running from the city to Dungarvan. Lorcan doesn't care about the exercise, he's indulging a lifelong fascination with locomotives, railways, and viaducts in particular. Joanne finds this endearing.

Inside the house, a door bangs and is immediately followed by a scream. She drops the towel she's folding and rushes in. Lorcan is standing, hands on hips, in the narrow hallway, where Marianne is crouched low with her back against the wall. She is cradling her hand and sobbing. Ella is in the bathroom doorway, shouting.

'I didn't do it! It was the wind –'

'There is no wind,' Joanne says.

'She did it on purpose,' Marianne wails.

Lorcan sends Ella to her room and coaxes Marianne off the floor and into the bathroom.

'I'll deal with this,' he says.

Joanne nods and goes back outside.

*

The first night of their holiday was so clear they'd sat outside with mugs of tea, watching shooting stars zip like silver bullets across the sky. Tramore, with its fast food takeaways and tacky arcades wasn't Joanne's choice. She would have preferred the tranquillity of the West – Achill Island or the Dingle Peninsula – but Lorcan had talked her around. There was so much to do with the girls: the beach, the amusements, the Greenway. 'Happy kids mean happy parents,' he'd said. Gentle persuasion was Lorcan's way. He'd a habit of getting what he wanted without having to ask for it. He could 'sell snow to the Eskimos' was how his brother had put it in the best man speech at their wedding.

Joanne half fills her glass with wine. Below her on the cliff walk she can hear teenagers. They are egging each other on. Probably to drink, or smoke or get off with somebody they fancy, or somebody they don't. Spin the bottle until it stops and you've to kiss the person it points to. Nearly thirty summers ago the bottle landed on Joanne, and before she had time to object Trevor Boyle's hard white tongue was invading her mouth. What was it with teenagers and their urge to fuck and torment each other? The next time Joanne felt so primal, she was bare-arsed to the world, as Marianne's head ripped her insides out. The nurse who'd sewn her back together wouldn't tell her how many stitches. 'An elective section next time, pet,' was all she'd say.

On the picnic table, Lorcan's mobile phone vibrates. She glances at the screen and catches a text message.

— Call me

It disappears before she sees who has sent it. Joanne has the phone in her hand when another text arrives. It is from 'T'.

— I need you. xx

She puts the phone on the table, picks up the towels and the wine, and walks towards the house, meeting Lorcan at the back door. He tells her the girls are in bed. Marianne's thumb doesn't look too bad.

'Right,' Joanne replies.

'I'm having a sneaky smoke,' Lorcan says, 'and I'll be in.'

The bed still smells of sex. Joanne lies with her back to him. He drifts off and she listens to the puffing sound his lips make when he snores. She does not sleep, not really. She flips through all the women she's ever met whose names begin with the letter T. Therese. Tríona, Tara. Joanne hasn't particularly warmed to any of them. Maybe it's a foreign name. Tamara. Or Tallulah.

Lorcan and Tallulah up a tree;
K-I-S-S-I-N-G.

He is not the type to sleep with a work colleague. Lorcan knows better than to shit where he eats. Maybe this is why Joanne doesn't mind as much as she should — that and the fact that she'd once been seduced into a six-week affair of frantic on-campus shagging until her co-adulterer, Professor Daniel Shapiro, cultural sociologist and renowned philanderer, went back to NYU, never to be heard from again.

She'd made full sure Lorcan never found out, and that's what bothers her now. The insolence of the texts. Does this woman think Lorcan is single? Separated, maybe? No. Joanne is sure 'T' knows the situation. It wounds her that Lorcan hasn't picked somebody more discreet, somebody less demanding, that he hasn't the decency to protect their marriage. She'd have no bother hacking into his phone to find out more. They have the same pin code, 2002: Marianne's birth year. Really, if he wants to fuck around, he should have the gumption to get a . . . what's it called? A burner phone? A cheap pay-as-you-go job that neither his wife nor his children would ever come across.

She watches the dawn grow brighter through the flimsy curtain. It's almost six o'clock when she slides out of bed and goes to the kitchen to make herself a cup of instant coffee and steal a cigarette from Lorcan's jacket. She unbolts the back door and walks across the grass to the picnic table. The dew feels good beneath her feet. Far out in the bay, there's a small white boat scudding across the water. Joanne watches and waits for it to disappear. Her throat tightens with the first drag of the cigarette, she stifles a cough, and after a slurp of coffee, the rest of the smoke is smooth. A wispy little fly has landed in her cup, its wings are bigger than its body. They are drenched and too heavy to lift. Soon it will drown.

*

117

At the breakfast table, Ella overpours the milk on her Cheerios. It runs across the table and drips on to the floor, where it pools in the cracks between the boards. She ignores the puddle beneath her bowl and continues eating her cereal. Joanne watches this and thinks how as a child she would have jumped up and looked for a cloth to clean the mess, how her fear of punishment made her apologetic, and how if she didn't appear sorry enough, she earned herself a slap. Ella, who is eight and does not regret slamming a door on her older sister's hand, has never felt the sting of a slap. Joanne fantasizes about pulling the child off the chair and smacking her hard across the back of her legs.

One, two, three times for hurting your sister.

Four, five, because you're not sorry.

Six and seven, for spilling milk and not cleaning it up.

The first few slaps are satisfying, but then Joanne feels ashamed. Worried that she herself might cry, she grabs a dishcloth from the draining board and begins to mop the milk up from the floor.

In the bathroom, the motor on the electric shower has been whirring for so long that she knows Lorcan is masturbating. When he's finished, he'll leave his towel on the floor. It'll lie there like a sleeping dog until Joanne picks it up. She would like to use the toilet, but he has locked the door, so she goes down the hall to check on Marianne and finds her lying on the top bunk, reading. She climbs to the third rung and tugs on the duvet.

'Hey, little bookworm.'

118

'Hi.'

'How's the thumb?'

'It hurts.' Marianne holds out her hand. The thumb-nail is split and the flesh beneath it is the colour of raw tuna. 'I don't want to go on the bikes,' she says.

Joanne cannot believe how much Lorcan under-played the thumb, as if it were a paper cut or a cat scratch. She'll have to take Marianne to the chemist for antibiotic powder and a dressing. She will lose the nail, you can tell by looking at it.

'Can I stay here with you today?'

Placing a hand on Marianne's forehead, she says, 'Of course.'

When Joanne tells Lorcan to head off on his own with Ella, he doesn't argue, even though he looks like he wants to. Rid of him, she flicks the radio on and begins to clean up after breakfast. There is no dish-washer. Really, there ought to be a dishwasher. She wipes the toast crumbs off the worktop, they land on the floor and she sweeps them, along with the sand they've carried from the beach in their shoes, into a dustpan that she empties in the swingbin beneath the sink. Down the town there are hotels where guests are served fry-ups with toast in a rack and tea in stainless-steel pots, where children squabble over miniature Kellogg's boxes and mash Coco Pops and Frosties into sweet brown sludge.

Joanne decides she will not make lunch for Mari-anne today, she'll buy chips on the Promenade.

*

They sit in the shade on the slip and watch the tide drag away from the shore. Marianne picks from the chip bag with her left hand. The pharmacist has dressed her right thumb with white gauze. 'I hate Ella,' she says. A group of children are playing a little further down the strand. They dig a shallow trench with their plastic spades, the biggest boy lies in it and the others cover him with sand until his body is a grey bulge and only his head pokes out. They use their hands and spades to hollow out a moat around him, the smaller children run back and forth to the sea, filling their buckets with water. Joanne envies the boy who has been buried alive.

'Would you like to play with those kids?'

'Maybe.' Marianne squints, her small white teeth press into the fat of her bottom lip. She considers it for a moment, then says, 'No.'

Joanne empties their leftover chips on to the rocks. The gulls screech and carry the scraps away. She twists the paper bag and stuffs it into her backpack. The beach, according to Marianne, is five kilometres long. 'I looked it up on the internet,' she says. They take their sandals off and walk along the shoreline in the last cold fizz of the broken waves. Though she tries not to, Joanne finds herself appraising the bodies of other women. They are stretched out on the sand, or carrying toddlers on their hips over rocky patches. Some, but not many, go into the sea. Joanne reckons she is doing well for her age. Her breasts sag a little, but the rest of her is firm, no thickening of the waist, or flattening of the behind. Her skin is pale and freckled, she waxes, she tints, she paints her toenails. She still wears her hair long, and when the occasion calls for it, she puts on make-up. Nothing drastic or desperate. Joanne is forty-two in September, she is beyond all that.

She checks her mobile phone and sees a text from Lorcan. It says they are eating ice cream on the Promenade.

'Daddy's back,' she tells Marianne, and they begin to weave their way through the sunbathers towards the strip of cafés that line the seafront. She spots him near the lifeguard hut, walking with Ella on his shoulders.

Lorcan sees her and he waves. 'Come on, we've tickets for the circus.'

Of course there is a circus. Joanne hadn't noticed the Big Top. The red and yellow stripes blend seamlessly into the gaudy diorama of the town. It bemuses her that some people consider circus an art form. But right now, she is open to anything that postpones for a couple more hours the requirement to talk to her husband.

Stepping into the tent is like entering a cave. The air feels cool and earthy, the smell of animal droppings is so pungent Joanne feels the urge to check her shoes for shit. Her eyes struggle to adjust to the darkness as the children stumble and bump their way on to the ringside benches. The floor of the ring is covered in straw and sawdust, there are clumps of horse dung, flattened into medallions, and matted fletches of straw where the animals have pissed.

While Lorcan is over buying bottles of Coke at the refreshment stand, the tent is plunged into blackness, and the PA system begins to crank out Shakira. In the control room, some unseen hand flicks a switch. Red, white and blue spotlights dance around the ring to the pulse of 'Hips Don't Lie'. Joanne is revising her opinion of the song, when it cuts out mid-chorus, and a contrived gypsy voice, a booming basso alto, announces that the show is about to begin.

By the time Lorcan makes it back to his seat, a palomino pony is trotting around the ring with a poodle on its back. Soon it is joined by one, two, three more ponies: sleek brown creatures that are mounted with a running jump by young lads in leather waistcoats, who ride standing up, backwards, any which way they can. Hooves stamp and pound the ring in a full-speed final lap. The earth trembles beneath them. Lorcan wolf-whistles as the horses and their riders exit the ring. They are replaced by a squat man in a tuxedo. He has with him a pair of albino parrots. One of the birds pushes a miniature shopping trolley up and down a plank of wood, while the other chirps, 'Hurry up, hurry up!' The children laugh and clap at this, and even Joanne is impressed when the trolley pusher, tired of being ordered around, tells the other parrot to, 'Shut up, shut up.'

There are dancing dogs, and a crocodile on a leash that does what it is told in exchange for raw chicken strips. Then comes a middle-aged punk rolling back and forth on a barrel as he swallows a sword. His side-kick, a rough-looking ticket with a purple Mohican and polio callipers on her legs, marches around him, juggling fire and kicking up sawdust. The paraffin fumes are nauseating and Joanne is glad when twin trapeze artists drop from the rigging, and spin like dia-manté spiders through the air. Ella watches intently, her mouth a small pink 'o'.

At the interval, Lorcan lines up with other parents and pays ten euro for Ella to do a circuit of the ring on a pony. A trapeze twin holds the rope that leads the one she's riding. Ella looks haughty on the circus horse, her deportment is pure dressage. Marianne doesn't want to ride. 'I can't bend my thumb,' she whines. Joanne hopes it won't always be like this. They are each other's only sibling.

When Ella's ride is over, she pesters Lorcan for another go. He shakes his head, but she persists. Mak-ing his stern face, he sweeps her out of the saddle and plants her on the ground in a move so effortless and swift she does not have time to protest. Ella stomps away from him, towards the gate, which is guarded by a clown in a paint-splattered boiler suit. There's a mar-moset monkey sitting on his shoulder and he's feeding it nuts from a toy plastic bucket. The clown winks at Ella, who, to Joanne's dismay, plunges her hand into the bucket and snatches a handful of nuts. The mon-key pounces on her. Then, just as quick, leaps back on to the clown's shoulder. Joanne springs from her seat, but Lorcan is already racing out of the tent with Ella in his arms.

'It fucking bit her.' Lorcan is puce. 'Fuck. Fuck. *Fuck*,' he says.

Marianne looks stricken that her father is cursing so freely in front of them. Nobody from the circus comes to see if Ella is okay. Joanne doesn't care, she just wants Lorcan to let go of the child so she can see for herself how bad it is. His T-shirt, dark with sweat, is stuck to his back. He's on his knees in the dust, with Ella pressed against his chest, and she is sobbing.

'Mummy. I want Mummy.'

Lorcan releases her.

'Let's have a look,' Joanne says, hunkering down and gently turning Ella's hand over in her own. She unfolds the short quivering fingers and sees there are two small holes where the monkey fangs have punctured Ella's skin. It's a nip, but there is blood. She presses a ball of tissue into her daughter's fist.

'You'll be fine, but you and me will go to the hospital just to be sure. Okay, love?'

Ella bawls. Marianne asks if she'll have to get an injection and be put in quarantine. Joanne tells Marianne to shush. Lorcan promises to bring everyone out for pizza and ice cream later – his treat.

'Will they shoot the monkey?' Marianne wants to know.

At the hatch in Accident and Emergency, Joanne gives their health insurance number to a surly woman whose face is so fat it appears to be eating her glasses.

'Date of birth?'

'Fifth of June, 2004.'

'Have you been here before?'

'We're on holidays.'

The fat woman repeats, 'Have you been here before?'

Joanne concedes that she has not and is handed a form on a clipboard to complete. The pen is almost out of ink. It's covered in Sellotape and hangs from the board by a hairy string. Joanne fills out the form and they're directed to a waiting room, where a dozen people sit with their backs to the wall on chairs that are screwed into the floor.

Judge Judy is on mute on a television high up in the corner. The plaintiff is a middle-aged bottle-blonde with breast implants. The defendant, a young Hispanic man, tugs on his tie. Joanne squints at the subtitles and learns that he is, in fact, the woman's husband. Judge Judy waves her hands in exasperation at the pair of them, she throws her eyes up to heaven, and brings her gavel down hard. Case dismissed. Outside the courtroom the defendant admits he's still in love with the plaintiff, who flicks her yellow hair and says she's willing to give him one more chance. Joanne imagines them in bed together, the sex is transactional. The thought of it depresses her. There's a commercial break and the patients shift in their moulded plastic seats. Slack-jawed, they watch ads for milk formula, car insurance and probiotic yoghurt.

Joanne sees, but tries not to look at, the couple sitting opposite. A man, a very drunk man, is holding a blood-soaked tea towel to his head. The woman with him is young enough to be his daughter but, by the stylish cut of her clothes, looks more like his solicitor. Ella is transfixed. Joanne doesn't like the way the woman is holding her daughter's gaze. She lowers her head and whispers into Ella's ear that it's rude to stare. Sitting up again, she catches the woman's eye, and still the woman does not look away. There's a defiance in her expression that frightens Joanne. For want of something to do, she texts Lorcan to say they've arrived at the hospital, but are still waiting to be seen. Then she scrolls through her emails, and her Face-book page.

The Tannoy crackles – 'Maurice Grant to triage' – and the staring woman helps the drunken man to his feet. Joanne is relieved to see them go.

The minutes pass. Ella leans into her and they watch the television. *Judge Judy* ends and a quiz show comes on. Joanne watches the contestants slam on their buzzers. She can tell by the scoreboard that they are useless, and she's glad she can't hear the stupid answers they give. A text notification sounds on her phone. Ella jumps and Joanne turns the volume down.

– *Sorry Babe, was I useless?*

– *No comment*

– *I'll make it up to you*

She doesn't respond.

He texts again.

– *I promise*

Joanne opens the YouTube app on her phone and finds a cartoon for Ella. The waiting room is full now. She wonders what diseases they have. Some are surely dying, most look too young or too old, or too uneducated, to understand what's wrong with them. Joanne wishes she could take Ella to a SwiftCare clinic. She considers for a mad moment getting into the car and driving home to Dublin.

A Traveller and her daughter have taken the seats opposite them. The child is lying across the woman's lap, her cheeks are florid, but her lips are pale and the skin around her mouth is blue. The girl picks at the sequins on her mother's leggings. New people arrive and it disgusts Joanne that they choose to stand, rather than sit beside the Travellers.

'Poor little mite,' she says.

'Asthma,' the woman replies, stroking the girl's hair. She glances at Ella and says, 'Is that your young one?'

Joanne nods, and realizing the woman is waiting for more information, she adds, 'A monkey bit her.'

Ella is too engrossed in Pokémon to notice how every head in the room has turned to look at her. Joanne tells the woman about the circus and the clown.

'Ye should make them put that monkey down,' the woman says. 'I got bit by a cat when I was pregnant.'

'Oh.'

'Yeah, on the mount of Venus —' the woman opens her palm to show Joanne the scar — 'the fat bit there, that's what they go for. Cats in anyway. I couldn't tell ye about monkeys.'

They stop talking and the waiting room is quiet but for the wheeze of the Traveller child, and the rattle in her chest when she coughs.

The Tannoy calls Bernard Buggy to triage, and everybody watches an obese man in a navy tracksuit rise from his seat and limp out of the room.

Joanne looks at her feet and notices the varnish on her big toenail is chipped. It doesn't matter. She will not clutter her mind with negative and unhelpful thoughts. These people around her, she won't see or think about them again. Just as 'T', who arrived unbidden, will never be let in. Joanne will leave this hospital and close a door on all of that. They won't ever return to Tramore. Allowing her gaze to drift over the poured resin floor, she contemplates the pale blue colour, flecked with silver like confetti, industrial yet pretty. Herself and Lorcan had priced something similar for the kitchen extension, but it was too expensive. In the end, they'd settled for Marmoleum. And honestly, after living with it for a while, she'd come to think it was the right choice.

The Fear

Jenny liked to get some air before her afternoon house calls. Most Tuesdays, she'd drive down to the Prom for lunch at Caruso's, where she'd sit at an outside table with a good view of the beach. She liked to watch the kite surfers, admire the 'fuck you' rhythm of their boards skipping across the water. No matter how hard she squinted, she could never make out the strings that bound them to their kites; every time they caught a gust of wind, she felt her heart soar at the fluorescent yellow slash marks they made across the sky. But today was a windless sort of day. There wouldn't be any kite surfers. The sky hung dull as pewter above the bay, and the sea had a grief-stricken look that she wasn't able for. It wouldn't have taken much to pull her under, not with the head she'd on her.

They were breeding like rabbits in the new estates beyond the racecourse, and she was flat out, haranguing first-time mothers about the benefits of breastfeeding, making sure they were getting their babies to latch on, and that they didn't have mastitis. Jenny was one of two public health nurses assigned to Tramore. The other, Mary Dunphy, was on compassionate leave for an undisclosed illness that everyone presumed to be her nerves. It was hard to be sympathetic. With the way things were, who wasn't suffering? The government had bailed out the banks, and now there was no money for anything, not even incontinence pads for her old and handicapped clients. When Jenny turned on the news, she was confronted by a government minister shaking his well-fed head and telling the country it had lost the run of itself, how stupidity and extravagance would cost us dearly for 'generations to come', but to remember – and be thankful – this was Ireland and not Greece. Greece was fucked. What good was all that civilization when they were up shit creek without a paddle?

Jenny wasn't so sure. The Greek finance minister was too handsome for politics, he drove around European summits on a gleaming motorbike, forever giving the IMF the finger. His name was Yanis. It had a strong, sexy ring to it, and Jenny liked his style. Besides, what had those beaky IMF shitehawks ever done for her? Except cut her pay and slap a recruitment ban on the health service, which meant she now had to cover Mad Mary's home visits on top of her own. And the upshot? If your post-partum fanny was healing too slowly, or your mind wandered up to The Metal Man to consider the pros and cons of throwing your body off the cliffs, PHN Jenny Supple had neither the time, nor the patience, to deal with your untreatable complaints. In fact, they weren't worth the cost of putting diesel in her '05 Ford Fiesta.

She took the bypass around the town. Known locally as 'the new road', it looped past housing developments and schools, and seemed to promise countryside, only to end abruptly at a roundabout. The first exit, a dirt track that led to the ghost estate, was sealed off by a row of black and amber bollards. Jenny took the second exit. It landed her in four tarmacadamed acres of rezoned farmland, freshly sliced and painted into a few hundred parking spaces, around which were planted: a Lidl, a 24-hour Tesco, and a private health centre with a team of general practitioners, a physio and a psychotherapist. There was a new credit union with an ATM that was forever 'out of service'.

Jenny decided to buy her lunch in the supermarket, and to recycle the wine bottles that were rolling around in the car boot while she was at it.

Supermarket shopping always carried the risk of running into clients. She rarely recognized them but they always spotted and cornered her, greedy for a bit of bonus care. They were surprised, offended even, when she appeared more interested in a tray of minced beef or a special offer on Listerine than she was in an update on their veins and their ulcers and their haemorrhoids. Once she left the context of their houses, they became strangers – she remembered them by their furniture, not their faces. 'Purple Velvet Curtains' was driven demented by a teething baby who'd neither sleep nor eat. 'Man with Slow Wall Clock' had diabetes and often farted with fright when she injected his belly. 'Black Leather Recliner' would kill himself by Christmas, unless the cancer got there first. You could never avoid them completely, but you could cut the odds by steering clear of the aisles that stocked nappies and alcohol.

'Black Leather Recliner' was one of her clients, not Mary's. She'd been calling on him for years. His name was Maurice Grant. And even though it was against the rules, Jenny brought him three large pouches of Amber Leaf tobacco every Tuesday, to save him going up the town. Drink, to which he had a lifelong devotion, she did not procure. His landlord did that. 'A right latchico' was how Maurice described him. For five euro commission, he'd drive up and down to Lidl, filling his hatchback with spirits and cans that he'd deliver to anyone who was too old, too sick or just too pissed to walk up the hill. Whiskey was Maurice Grant's poison, and there was always a bottle beside his recliner when she called.

Tobacco bought, Jenny walked around the supermarket with her earphones in, listening to the radio on her mobile. One of those blokes-telling-jokes kind of shows, all celeb gossip, cat music and listeners texting the presenters as if they were good mates who'd run into each other in Supermac's last Saturday night. They were on about some Hollywood actor who'd been diagnosed with throat cancer after he'd contracted the HPV virus through oral sex. 'It's scary,' one of the jocks said, 'nobody knew it could affect men.' Serves ye right, Jenny thought. Picking up a plastic bowl of salad Niçoise, she examined the contents: the egg yolk was going grey, it had a black rim around it; the tuna looked parched, and she counted just one, two, three black olives, like little knobs of sheep shit. She put the salad back on the shelf and moved along the fridges past the Tesco Finest pork pies and sausage rolls. People go mad for pastry. *Samosas: authentic Indian street food; spiced potato in a crispy shell.* Oh the joys of being single, you could eat whatever and whenever you wanted. She'd stayed away from meat for the five years she was with Gerard. He wouldn't have it in the house, and – not counting the odd blaa with ham or luncheon sausage at work – she too had abstained. Was there any chance she'd given Gerard the HPV virus? It was no more than he deserved. She picked up a chicken tikka sandwich and brought it to the cashier.

Nobody interrupts when you eat lunch in your car. There's no 'Do you mind if I join you?' or 'Is there anyone using this chair?' No need to wipe your chin, or discreetly suck lettuce from between your teeth. You just put up the windows and lock the doors.

My lunch.

My car.

Fuck off, world.

As she took one final, unsatisfying bite of her sandwich, a coffin dodger in an Auris pulled in beside her. Jesus Christ, there was nothing but empty spaces in the car park, loads of them at the supermarket entrance, and loads more beside the trolley bay. He hauled his bones out of the car and locked it, then he bent down and peered in her passenger window. Was he a client? Jenny swung her head in the opposite direction and watched, with great interest, a woman coming out of the credit union. She was dressed in a navy waistcoat and A-line skirt, with white sports socks and runners on her feet. She stopped at a sign that said 'TALK TO US TODAY ABOUT A LOAN' and dragged it into the credit union. When the door swung behind her, she flipped the sign to 'CLOSED'.

Jenny got out of the car and took the empties from her boot. The mouth of the bottle bank was full of Buckfast; as she pushed the empty wine bottles in, broken glass crunched beneath her feet. This was it, she concluded, the darkest hole in Ireland. Was it any wonder Maurice Grant didn't want to leave the house? He'd be able for it alright. Most of the ones on the public health round were diabetic, middle-aged men and women whose privates were buried beneath their three-stone bellies, and because they could only cover short distances with a flat-footed shuffle that winded them, it was easier to stay housebound. Maurice was nimble. The kind that never carried much weight, he'd a gaunt look since the diagnosis. He was clean-shaven, with trimmed sideburns and greying hair Brylcreemed into a quiff. His clothes were spruce enough to be seen in, but the only people Maurice ever saw were his landlord, his daughter Helen, and, on Tuesday afternoons, Jenny.

She remembered how, a few months back, it occurred to her that he must have been good-looking when he was younger. And how, on the same day, she noticed the house had been cleaned; particles of sunlight poured through the kitchen window and bounced off the stainless-steel draining board. Her feet didn't stick to the lino, and there was a mirror she hadn't seen before above the mantelpiece. Not only had Maurice's Waterford crystal ashtray been emptied, it sparkled on the padded arm of his black leather recliner. That's when it struck her, the house looked and smelled better, not him.

'You've the place looking lovely,' she said.

'That'd be Helen,' he replied. 'Forever interfering.'

'Right.'

He winked. 'I'd be lost without her.'

It would be a year before he'd need the hospice, and when he did, she'd have another added to her list in his place. Somebody she liked less. Maybe she should get him his whiskey. Who would know – and what did Maurice have to lose anyhow? The only person missing out would be his racketeering landlord.

Twenty to two. She still had time. Jenny grabbed her handbag off the passenger seat and headed for Lidl, where she bought a bottle of Dundalgan and a gift bag.

She was having second thoughts by the time she took the turn-off for the Prom. Ropes of cloud squeezed what light there was out of the sky. Maybe Maurice would be peeved that she'd crossed some unspoken boundary? Tobacco was fine, he'd asked for it. But whiskey? That was a different matter entirely. She decided to leave the bottle in the car and see what kind of form he was in. She could get it once she'd checked his prescriptions had been filled and his blood pressure was normal. All casual, she would say it'd been given to her as a gift, but that she'd no taste for spirits.

Jenny rang the doorbell. Through the bubbled glass, the lamp on the hall table gave off a jaundiced light. Maurice Grant's porch was always littered with bills and flyers; a soggy pile of fast food menus, freesheets, and cards telling him he'd missed the meter reader, again. He'd open the door and use the toe of his shoe to shunt them behind a flower pot filled with fag ends. Jenny rang the bell again. She thought about gathering the junk mail and putting it in the wheelie bin beneath the front window, but that would be taking liberties. There was still no sign of him. She slid the door open, stepped into the porch and rapped on the glass. It sometimes happened that clients didn't answer their doors, either because they were out, or because they weren't in the mood. Maurice never did this. Even if he didn't want to see her, he wanted his tobacco, and for that alone he'd let her in. Jenny rooted for her mobile and called him. She listened to his phone ring out through the warped frame of the front room window.

Back in the car, Jenny moved the gift bag from the passenger seat to the floor, and flipped through her files. Maurice's next of kin was his daughter. Helen Grant's number was scratched in faded Biro on the Health Board consent form. Her mobile went straight to voicemail. Jenny left a message and waited a few minutes before texting.

– *Hi, it's your dad's PHN, he's not answering the door. Just checking all is OK?*

She hit send and then, swiping at the screen, stalled on the words *Gerard. Mobile. 11 hrs ago.*

The night before came back to Jenny in sickening instalments: Facebook open on the laptop. The second bottle of wine. Melissa spitting down the phone. 'It's three in the morning. Leave us the fuck alone!' The baby had started to cry. Jenny imagined his tiny pink face swaddled in a blanket between them on the bed. Gerard, the scabby bastard, had probably refused (on environmental grounds) to buy a new mattress.

He took the phone from Melissa. 'You have to stop,' he said. 'It's not fair.'

Fair? Since when was anything fair? That was the problem with Gerard, he was all about justice. The smug bastard wouldn't know fairness if it slapped him in the face.

'You were my husband first.' She'd thought it, but had she actually said it? She blanched at the realization that she had.

'Get help,' he said, and hung up.

Jenny pushed back the car seat and closed her eyes. She listened for the soothing roll and crash of the waves, but it did not come. Her heart was trying to punch its way out of her ribcage. Blood thumped through her veins. She was going to overheat, her brain felt too big for her skull, something was about to crack. There would be a terrible mess. She counted backwards from a hundred and did her breathwork.

This too shall pass.

A car door slammed. She sat up and looked around. A woman of about her own age, tall with dark cropped hair, was standing at Maurice's front door. She struggled for a moment with the key, and went inside.

Jenny got out of the car. By the time she reached the porch, Helen Grant was back in the doorway, blocking it. Her mouth stretched tight across her bloodless face like a scar.

Jenny understood. She reached into her coat pocket and took out her phone.

'Will you tell them he's dead?' she said as she closed the door.

They waited together for the ambulance to arrive and, separated by glass, they cried.

St Otteran's

Nanny Moll came gusting across the green with a headscarf knotted tight beneath her chin. She'd a carrier bag pressed against her bosom, and the tail of her raincoat flapped out behind her like bedsheets in a gale. I stood at the bedroom window, watching through the net curtains as I pulled up my tights. The front door clicked open and, caught by a draught, it banged shut again. Nanny had arrived. She shuffled down the hall and complained that the wind outside would skin a bastard cat.

'Helen!' Mam shouted, and I came downstairs.

Last week's *Munster Express* was laid out on the kitchen table, Mam was polishing my school shoes, the brush in her hand flew back and forth in a sooty blur. Nanny, still in her scarf and coat, sat in her usual chair by the fireplace, with a mug of tea on the mantelpiece, and a fag in her hand. She always let the ash get so long I thought it would fall into her lap, but it never did, at the last minute she'd bend forward, tap on the cigarette, and the grey bit would drop softly into the grate.

She took a quick drag. 'Well, girl, are you looking forward to seeing your dada?'

I was, of course. Dada had been away working since

before Halloween but then he'd an accident on the site – he was up on the scaffold when a wheelbarrow of bricks fell and split him open, so he'd to go to hospital inside in the town. He'd been too sore to see anyone except Nanny and Mam, but he was well enough now for me to visit too, and, with a bit of luck, he'd be home in time for Christmas.

Nanny pulled the hem of my pinafore so that the corduroy lines were straight.

'Did you make a nice card for your dada, Helen?'

'It's there on the table,' said Mam.

Nanny picked up the card and looked at the drawing I did of me, Mam and Christy, with the words '*Get Well Soon*' written above our heads. She smacked her lips. 'Isn't that grand?' she said, putting the card into her bag. 'Now, have you all your news?'

I tried to keep things in the order they'd happened – reciting my news, as she ate her slice of buttered bread.

'I got nineteen out of twenty in my spellings.'

Nanny nodded in a way that I knew to go on.

'Muriel Power's cat had kittens and when they're big enough, she's giving me a black one and it's going to live in the coal shed.'

Mam came up behind me with a hairbrush. She put her hand on top of my head and the bristles felt divine running through my hair and down my back. My hair was full of static that made it crackle and cling like a magic trick to the sleeve of Mam's blouse. With long strokes of the brush, she scooped my hair up into a ponytail. The go-go she was holding between her teeth made her voice sound all funny when she spoke, like a ventriloquist, or someone whose lips had been sewn together.

'Don't forget about Halloween,' she said.

That set me off about the barmbrack, and how I got the ring, Christy got the matchstick, and Mam got the pea. She wound the go-go around my ponytail.

And I said, 'We're going to Shaw's after school on Wednesday to see Santy.'

Nanny tongued the bit of turnover she'd been chewing into her cheek. Then, out the corner of her mouth, she told me to go out into the hall and put on my coat. I knew they didn't want me to hear what they were on about, because herself and Mam were talking in shushy voices. I stood by the front door, pulled up my hood and tied the string into a bow.

J. J. Hennebry's bus was late and there were loads of people crowded into the shelter trying to stay dry. But it was no good because the rain was coming sideways from the sea instead of down out of the sky, hard salty sheets of it pelting all the people in their winter coats, on their way into town to do their Christmas shopping. A man with a silver snot dripping out of his nose got up off the bench to let Nanny sit down, and when the bus came along the kerb he stood aside to let us on before him. We sat near the back, where the seats were nice and hot. I could feel the engine grumble beneath me until the doors snapped shut, and away we went into town.

Nanny didn't speak until the conductor took our fares. She handed me the curly paper ticket, and said I was to put it into my pocket and keep it safe. The smell of wet coats was making me feel sick. I wiped the window with my sleeve, looked out at the cardboard-coloured sky, and practised my news for Dada. People got on at every stop. It felt like hours had passed by the time we arrived at the big bus station that Nanny called 'the end of the line'. It was manners to let the other people off first. I watched them cross the road and take off down the quay in little groups, before they vanished into the shops, all glittery with Christmas lights.

We walked along the riverbank holding hands. At Reginald's Tower Nanny stopped and pointed up into the sky. 'Can you see it, Helen? Cromwell's cannonball stuck into the wall?'

I squinted and said that I could. She asked me if I knew the story of Strongbow and Aoife. I pretended I couldn't remember, and she pretended not to have told me it a dozen times before, so that she might tell me again, and I would 'ooh' and 'ahh' at the best parts.

'And now,' she said, 'half of Waterford is descended from the Normans, on account of Aoife being given to Strongbow.'

'To keep the peace,' I reminded her.

'That's it, girl,' said Nanny, 'to keep the peace.'

In The People's Park, a man was kissing a woman in the bandstand. Nanny got cross and gave out to me for gawking at them. We went into the Tip Top sweet shop and she bought a bottle of Lucozade in gold crinkly plastic, and a quarter of bullseyes that she slipped into her coat pocket.

Dada was in a different hospital than the one where I was born, and where my brother Christy had his appendix out. Dada's hospital was hidden behind high walls that were covered in ivy, we'd to push hard against the rusted gates to make them open. Beyond them was a jungle of mahonia bushes in full bloom, the yellow flowers wet and droopy under their own weight. We took the stone path that led to the infirmary. Nanny banged the brass hard against the door and we waited for someone to come. There was a sign. A painted metal plaque that said: SAINT OTTERAN'S. It made me laugh. Nanny told me to stop acting the maggot or they wouldn't let us in to see Dada at all.

A nurse brought us to his room. She must have been a nun, as well as being a nurse, because Nanny kept calling her 'Sister'. The corridor she brought us down had a freckly pink floor that reminded me of fairy cakes. You could tell people were forever being sick or having the runs because there was a smell of Dettol, and they couldn't open the windows to let it out, because the windows were way up high on the walls and they had iron bars on them. I'd say they were nearly as high as Cromwell's cannonball.

Instead of a window Dada's room had a picture of the Sacred Heart of Jesus. He'd his own sink, a single bed like my one at home, and beside it, a wooden locker, where Nanny unloaded the contents of her carrier bag: the bottle of Lucozade, five boxes of Carroll's, a couple of cowboy books, and the card I was after making. Dada sat on the edge of the bed, smoking. He'd pyjamas on that he must have got especially for hospital because he normally went to bed in his underpants and vest. There was a tartan dressing gown on the back of the door and a pair of matching slippers on the floor. The pattern reminded me of the wrapper on the caramels he liked to eat, and I was sorry we didn't think to buy him some in the shop. Dada had grown a beard. He looked different, like someone I didn't know.

He picked my card up off the locker. 'That's a lovely picture. Did you do it yourself?'

I went all red. The room was too hot and I couldn't think of anything to say. When was he going to ask me about my news?

Nanny told me to take myself down the hall to the television room, she wanted 'a word' with Dada. 'I'll be down for you in a minute,' she said.

The television room was full of men watching a black and white war film. They were in their dressing gowns, and most of them were smoking, even the ones who looked like they were asleep. I sat down on a chair inside the door and one of the men said 'for fuck's sake' when he saw me. There was a nurse sitting on a low table in front of him, doing something to his feet, cutting his toenails, I think. She told him to be quiet, but he kept looking at me like he wanted to give me a clout, or something. I didn't like to look at him so I watched the film instead. German soldiers were shoving bombs into cannons and firing them at a boat full of English sailors. Bodies flew into the air and into the sea. They ran out of bombs, and took to using machine guns, cursing and swearing in German as they blew the English lads to smithereens. They were still at it when Nanny came to bring me back to Dada's room. He was ready now to hear my news, she said.

It went well enough, except he said that Muriel Power could keep her cats. Nanny had me sing a bit of 'Silent Night' for him in Irish, and when I finished Dada clapped his giant hands together.

'Bualadh bos,' he went. And then, 'Maith an cailín.' He'd such a peculiar look about him. 'Are you helping your mam?'

I was, I assured him. And, we'd be going to see Santy on Wednesday. Then I remembered the question Mam wanted me to ask.

'Will you be home for Christmas, Dada?'

He lit a cigarette and just as he was about to answer, Nanny jumped up and gave out stink to me. It was up to the doctor, she said. My father wasn't well and I wasn't to be bothering him with stupid questions.

'Make them fags last,' she said to Dada. And then, to me, 'Button your coat, missy.'

I followed her out of the room and did my best not to bawl in front of Dada. It wasn't fair, I was only doing what I was told. As I closed the door, he called me back.

'Tell your mam I'll be home,' he said.

It was dark when we got to Tramore. Nanny Moll was in better form and said we'd go down to the Prom to get our tea. She bought four singles with sausages and a bottle of red sauce. We walked home by the caravan park. The rain had stopped and the sea rolled gently on to the strand, above us the moon was round as a football floating through outer space. The chipper bag felt like a lovely hot-water bottle against me, Nanny stuck her hand into it and pulled out a few chips. The smell of vinegar was making me hungry, so she told me I could have some too. We ate them walking through the estate, our breath rising like great big chimney puffs into the night.

Christy let us in, and tore straight back up the stairs again. Mam was on the settee in the good room, with a string of fairy lights trailing across the carpet and over her knees; she was twisting the little bulbs, looking for the faulty one. On the floor by her feet was the Christmas tree, waiting for us to bend down the branches and twist the bristles into shape. All of a sudden, the bulbs lit up.

'There it is now,' said Mam.

She looked like a film star with the coloured lights brightening her face. That's when I saw the tea chest of decorations had been taken down from the attic. It was over by Dada's armchair. I was mad to get at them. But first we'd to go into the kitchen for our tea.

Mam slapped the bottom of the sauce bottle to make it come out. 'Well,' she said, 'how did ye get on?'

Nanny told her we got on grand.

'Maurice will be home for Christmas.'

Mam ate her chips.

'He told you that?'

'He told Helen, didn't he, pet?'

'He did.'

Mam reached over and tapped my hand. 'Call your brother down,' she said. 'After you finish your tea, you can go inside and start unwrapping the decorations.'

When Christy reached the foot of the stairs he punched me in the arm. A real deadener it was, but I didn't cry, or tell on him. I held my whist, finished my chips, and thought about doing the decorations. It was the best job in the world, rooting through the tea chest, peeling back the layers of old newspaper to find something fancy inside, and trying to guess if the next one I opened would be the holy angel for the top of the Christmas tree. Except for Mam, she was the most beautiful thing I'd ever seen.

The Machine

Marcus Mackey was doing her a favour. He knew it and she, Geraldine Halpin, also knew. He was about ten years older than her, with dead brown eyes and a soft belly that wobbled over the top of his stone-washed denims. He wore his hair in a rat's tail, tucked into the collar of his biker jacket. She'd watch out for him on rent day, pulling up on the kerb in his third- or fourth-hand Toyota Estate, always checking his reflection in the car window before he came to the door and rang the bell.

'It's fifty a week in cash – on top of the rent cheque,' he said when she moved in. 'Can you stretch to that?'

'Sure.' She handed him a Biro and the rent allowance form to sign.

'Are you from around here?'

'Originally.' She turned her back to him and opened the kitchen press. It was full of empty whiskey bottles.

'You can stick those in the recycling,' he said.

'Was the house not cleaned?'

Marcus Mackey ignored the question. He dropped the unsigned form on the worktop. 'And it's just yourself and your daughter?'

She nodded. Saoirse was stomping around upstairs, already Blu-tacking posters to the bedroom wall; the bassline of whatever she was listening to thumped on the kitchen ceiling.

'Are you into music yourself?' he asked.

'A bit.'

He gave her the once-over, not caring that she noticed when his eyes stalled on her breasts.

'I play a bit meself,' he said. 'In the hotel at the weekends.'

'Right.'

'Classics mostly. Don Henley and The Eagles, a bit of Zeppelin or The Doors.' He leaned across to sign the form. 'I can put your name on the door.'

'Thanks.'

'If there's a problem with the house, or anything, I'm on the mobile.'

She asked him to get rid of the black recliner that was pocked with cigarette burns, it had sponge the colour of rancid cheddar bursting through the ripped vinyl.

'Put it out in the yard,' he said.

She got a job cleaning at one of the guest houses. So long as she showed up on time and the work was done right, the owner, Muriel, was willing to pay her off the books. 'I know how it is, girl,' she said. Geraldine felt awkward asking, but didn't want to bump into her signing on in the post office. You couldn't get away with that sort of thing in a place like Tramore.

They'd been living in Waterford the previous year when Saoirse turned twelve. Suddenly she was all legs and they'd to go into Shaw's to have her fitted for a bra. She was getting looks, not from lads her own age, but from teenagers, and older men in cars. Geraldine watched them watching her, in her school jumper and skirt, the weight of her books dragging her back as she walked up the hill to the estate, key rings and bag charms jangling with each bouncy step. She knew then she'd never let her daughter walk up the road alone from school.

Tramore is seven miles out the road, but Saoirse says it feels 'like another country'. The sky is huge and full of gulls. When you step outside, the air tastes salty.

Before Geraldine goes to work, she puts a ham and coleslaw roll into her daughter's backpack, leaves a bowl of cereal on the kitchen table, and shouts up the stairs that it's time to get up for school. In the guest house, she turns around the rooms for early check-ins, stripping the beds and putting on fresh sheets and pillowcases. She runs a yellow duster over every surface and hoovers the carpet. In the en-suite, she rinses out the sink and the shower tray, always checking the plugholes for hair. The last thing she does is empty the bathroom bin, there's normally only a plastic razor or a couple of cotton buds in it. Sometimes a guest leaves a bloody sanitary towel. What kind of person does that?

Muriel offers her a cup of tea at the end of the shift.

It's nice of her, but Geraldine never takes it. On Mondays and Wednesdays, there's a Zumba class she goes to in Seascape Health and Fitness. On Tuesdays, she signs on. On Fridays, Muriel pays her two hundred euro for the week. She buys pepperoni pizzas in Lidl and a bottle of red wine that she drinks watching a movie on the sofa with Saoirse.

The washing machine broke five months after they moved in. It was in the middle of the spin cycle when the innards came undone, for a couple of minutes it appeared to be having a seizure, jumping up and down on the lino. The noise was unbelievable. It let off an almighty shudder, then a groan, before spluttering water from its undercarriage, and stopping dead. Geraldine waited a few minutes, then opened the door. Water gushed out, soaking her feet. She reached into the buckled metal drum and hauled the clothes out. Saoirse's school uniform flopped, black and heavy as a seal, on to the kitchen floor.

   – Hi Marcus, the washing machine is broken

Mackey didn't reply to her text. Not that evening, or for the rest of the week. Geraldine looked around the town but there was no launderette. As she hand-washed their clothes in the kitchen sink, she thought about how great it must be to live in America, like in *Friends*, where there's a laundromat on every corner. Clean-smelling places, with industrial-sized machines that wash and dry your clothes with futuristic power and speed. She would sit there reading a magazine or look out the window at the city buzzing by, while her neighbours folded their T-shirts and duvet covers into warm neat piles. There's community in laundromats, she thought. In Ireland, people had their own washing machines in their own houses. *Own*. They didn't own anything. She sent Mackey another text. He replied:

— *Tied up. Drop down to the hotel tomorrow nite?*

She told Muriel what'd happened and asked if she could wash Saoirse's school uniform in the guest house machine.

Muriel looked at her kind of squinty-eyed. 'Alright,' she said, 'but you know there's public machines outside the petrol station on the way into the town?'

'The Maxol?'

'Indeed, isn't the world gone half-cracked.'

The machines at the Maxol were on the forecourt, beside the Air, Vacuum and Water station. Inside was a café, a rectangle of parquet flooring laid out with brushed-steel tables and chairs, where you could drink coffee from the self-serve Frank and Honest machine as you watched your clothes spin and tumble in the giant portholes outside. It was hypnotic. Stupefying, in fact. When Geraldine got bored counting down the digits, waiting for her cycle to end, she watched cars pulling up to the petrol pumps and read their registration plates, to see who was local and who was not.

Waterford. Waterford. Dublin.

Wexford. Waterford, again.

Cork.

It cost ten euro to wash and dry a load at the garage. It was handy enough, and she might have given up asking Mackey to replace the machine, until she noticed the dank fungal aroma that attached itself to the fibres of Saoirse's school jumper.

'You smell like a wet dog.'

She jumped up from her homework, and stormed out of the room, roaring, 'Don't you start on me too.'

After a couple of hours, she came downstairs, her face all red and puffy from crying. They'd been barking and whistling at her in school, she said.

'Who's *they*?'

'Everyone.'

'Like who?'

'A young one in third year started it.'

'What's her name?'

'Amanda Duggan. She said I smell like a bitch in heat.'

'You tell that bibe I'll break her face if she starts on you again.'

Saoirse wore her blouse and skirt to school the next day and Geraldine brought the jumper up to the Maxol to complain about the smell of it. The girl on the counter shrugged.

'People put dog beds in the machine,' she said.

'That shouldn't be allowed.'

'It isn't,' she replied.

'You should put up a sign.'

The girl cast a jaded glance over Geraldine's shoulder, there was a queue forming behind her.

A few days later, she got a text from Mackey, saying he'd be down to look at the machine during the week. He never came.

— *Marcus, can you fix the machine?*

— *Marcus, will I get a new machine out of the rent?*

Muriel wasn't one bit surprised when she heard about the dog beds in the Maxol. 'Get that landlord of yours to fix the machine,' she said.

Geraldine did her washing in the guest house again that weekend. She didn't want to push her luck. It wouldn't be easy to come by another under-the-counter job, never mind work she could do while Saoirse was at school, or sleeping until midday at the weekend. She bought Muriel a bunch of Oriental lilies to assure her she wasn't the kind to take advantage.

— *Marcus, Harvey Norman have a machine on sale for 149 euro (plus delivery)*

She'd have bought it herself if she owned a credit card, but the lousy creep would inherit it when he kicked them out. They'd go, as they'd arrived, with everything they owned in the boot of a taxi.

She took to washing their clothes by hand in the bath, then hung them dripping on a clothes horse by the double radiator in the kitchen. The heat came on for an hour in the morning, and three in the evening. The washing started to smell before it started to dry; the window fogged up with condensation, and a rash of black mould appeared on the ceiling. One evening,

as she spooned pasta into bowls for their tea, Geraldine glanced over at Saoirse and the look on her face
was one of pure disappointment: at the state of the
place, at the cheap penne, at her mother.

'The house is damp,' was all she said.

It occurred to Geraldine that she'd been very unlucky
with the Maxol machines, she'd stuffed her washing in
just after somebody else had pulled their dog beds
out. She decided to give the place another go.

She'd eaten a jam doughnut and was almost finished her coffee, counting down the digits on the
tumble dryer, when a silver SUV pulled up in front
of the machines and blocked her view. A man got
out. He was carrying a pair of fleece dog beds,
each the size of a child's paddling pool. He tossed
them into the machine, inserted his coinage and was
walking back around his car by the time she inter-
cepted him.

'You're not allowed to put dog beds in the machines.'

The man looked her up and down. 'And who the
fuck are you?' He spat on the ground and pushed
roughly past her.

She watched him get into the car. As he slammed
the door, she threw the dregs of her coffee at his side
window. It dripped in milky rivulets down the glass.
Geraldine saw a child's face inside the car staring out
at her. A little boy of about two, his mouth clenched
around a bottle teat, and a halo of blond curls so wild
they looked like a wig.

The man lowered his window and, driving away, he shouted, 'Y'know, you're only a knacker.'

Behind her, the Maxol dryer gave three loud beeps. She took the washing out and held Saoirse's jumper to her nose. This time, it smelled alright.

Home

I took a Xanax soon as I woke up this morning. That's what going back to Tramore does to me. It starts the moment I book my flight. I drink and smoke too much (mostly cigarettes, but sometimes weed), and I hardly sleep. I just lie there and imagine my mother in the old folks' home, refusing to take her medication. Twice a year, I make the pilgrimage; once for Christmas, and once for my god-daughter Evie's birthday, in July. She scrawls the words '*Welcome Home, Auntie Stella*' on the driveway, in pink and blue chalk. It's kind of sweet.

I never stay more than a few days. And from the moment I get on the Tube in Brixton, it feels punitive, five stops to Green Park, another seventeen to Heathrow, the customary run for the loo when I arrive at the airport. A complete evacuation. Every single time. It sometimes feels like I've spent my entire life in transit at Heathrow, gaping slack-jawed at Kay Burley and Adam Boulton on Sky News. The birth of Prince George. The death of Amy Winehouse. The 2012 London Olympics. I watched all of these marooned on Pier 4. It's easy to spot the Irish in airports. Not just the ones in county colours, towing a string of sunburnt children, but the whole bockety lot of them, with their cheap suitcases and craven, hangdog heads, speed-smoking outside the terminal. Technically, Irish citizens don't need a passport travelling to and from the UK because, deep down, the English still think they own us. It doesn't matter how often you stick your harp-embossed passport under their noses, geographically speaking, Ireland is in the British Isles, the provincial poor relations, with their brassy highlights and muffin tops, rooting in Duty Free bags for boarding passes, spilling giant bars of Toblerone and cartons of Johnny Blue all over the floor. I find it hard to look at them without feeling something that borders on shame.

Last year, they moved the Irish flights to Terminal 2, confirmation that we've scrambled up the ladder of respectability in the English mindset. It's not the Pad-dies who are blowing the crap out of London now. I couldn't have lived here when they were. I was still in New York when 9/11 happened, and I remember how the loud and busy Zam Zam Deli on the corner of our block fell suddenly silent, the owner seemed to recoil in shame when you asked him for olives or baklava, adding more than you wanted, but charging you less. 'Sorry,' he said. 'I am very sorry.' I lost count of the apologies I heard from cab drivers and delivery guys, all of them Middle Eastern or Pakistani. On New Year's Eve 2001, the super of our building, an elderly Egyptian called Bassem, stepped off the platform at Borough Hall as a Coney Island-bound F train emerged from the tunnel. My neighbour told me afterwards, 'He wasn't even a Muslim.'

I got out at the right time. New York had been good to me. They gave me a Green Card, and when I was eligible for citizenship, I took that too. You could say America washed the muck off me. When I arrived in London, it didn't feel like I was just another bogtrotter from across the pond. Brixton was the closest thing to Brooklyn I could find, and eventually it came to feel like home.

My sister says our mother is 'spitting venom'. I can't tell any more if Tish is trying to warn me, or to guilt me. Seems to me Nancy always spat venom, was always *out* with somebody: Auntie Stasia, the next-door neighbour, my brother Michael and his 'appalling' wife. It's not easy to stay *in* with a person whose default position is disapproval.

My most exasperating defect was 'a soft spot for the underdog'. My husband Esteban, who she called 'The Mexican', even though he was Argentinian. Friends I made in school. Helen Grant and Ger Halpin – people who meant a lot to me – were low rent, according to her. 'Don't come crying to me,' she'd say, 'when they turn around and bite you.'

So I didn't. When Esteban and I split up, I said nothing, and not once did she ask me what happened to my husband. It was as if our marriage never existed – she annulled it, the minute she heard about it.

Heathrow Terminal 2 is basically a shopping mall. There's a *YO! Sushi* and a Heston Blumenthal café.

You can get a shoeshine, or a bikini wax, or pick up the latest issue of *Vogue*. In the Cath Kidston store I buy Evie a backpack and pencil case that are covered in tiny strawberries. I'm in Tish's bad books for not flying home when Evie made her Holy Communion, in May. The card I sent, with a £50 note, was not enough compensation. Should I get Tish a bottle of Jo Malone perfume? I probably should, and therefore I do. The one that smells like dandelions and Mr Sheen. I buy my brother-in-law 200 Marlboro Lights, which will immediately undo the goodwill generated by Cath Kidston and Jo Malone, because I should not be encouraging Marty to smoke. I'm still loitering in the Duty Free, spritzing my wrists with Chanel, when an Irish accent summons all remaining passengers for Dublin to the gate.

The woman beside me in Seat 12C (aisle) is wearing a duck-egg blue shirt that's so crisp I want to reach out and touch it. Her skin is tastefully tanned and, like her shirt, it's unwrinkled. There's a slender gold chain around her neck, a diamond solitaire dangles from it, sparkling. She doesn't want to talk. That's fine by me. I take another Xanax as the plane crawls up the queue for take-off. Over the PA, a voice identifying itself as Brian is going to be our pilot 'for the short flight to Dublin'. I don't understand the need for chit-chat from the cockpit. When I started travelling, hearing the pilot's voice was never a good thing, it meant turbulence, a bird strike or some imminent catastrophe.

The Tanqueray and tonic I order during the flight is

exquisite, as alcohol at 40,000 feet tends to be. I watch my neighbour's (unmarried) fingers peck the keyboard of her tiny laptop. Her manicure can't disguise the fact that she's a nail-biter.

I know that Marty will be waiting for me in the airport, that's what good husbands do: drive a five-hour round trip to pick up their sister-in-law. I'd be happy taking the InterCity bus, but Tish won't hear of it. And when we arrive in Tramore, she'll be pissed because she'd to work, and mind Evie, and visit Mum, and shop, and prepare the dinner on her own, because Marty was gone all day collecting me from the airport. It's always the same. I swear I'll take the bus next time, but I never do, because she insists I can't walk into the Arrivals hall and not be met, as if I belong to no one. Tish, I want to tell her, I don't belong to anyone.

When Tish and Marty got married, I was taking a year out with Esteban in Chiapas. I came back on my own for the wedding, wore the stupid dress she bought for me, and put up with being choreographed left and right, so my tattoos weren't visible in the photographs. Between that and Nancy's spaghetti western view of my marriage, I couldn't wait to leave Ireland. Things had been rocky with Esteban for a while. Still, I was shocked when, the morning after Tish's wedding, he sent an email saying he needed 'space to think about the future' and was going home to Buenos Aires. I should return to New York, he said, or Chiapas, if I preferred. He'd given back the keys of our rented house in San Cristóbal. My clothes and paintings were in storage at the Liberacion Café. The timing of the break-up stung. What a spineless bastard he was. I went back to New York, but my heart wasn't in it. I needed to make art, not fucking adverts. I hated graphic design and I hated waking up alone. Within six months, I'd sold the apartment in Brooklyn. I went to Cuba, where I cried and drank so much rum that, in the end, I couldn't tell whether Esteban or alcohol was the source of my misery. One hung-over morning, I walked past a travel agent, did a U-turn and, without giving it any thought, bought myself a one-way ticket to London.

I've always loved the descent into Dublin: Howth Head and Bull Island, the mouth of the Liffey and the Poolbeg chimney stacks. Why does this sweep of coastline make me feel elated? I've never even lived in Dublin. It must have something to do with the sudden drop in altitude because soon as the plane lands, the feeling's gone.

In the Arrivals hall, I don't recognize Marty and walk past him. He calls out, 'Stella!' and I turn around. He's grown a beard and his thinning hair has been shorn down to a grey fuzz. The Paul Smith shirt he's wearing was definitely a Tish purchase.

'You should've brought a sign.'

He laughs at this and leans in awkwardly to kiss my cheek. 'How's it goin'?'

'Grand,' I say. 'Thanks for picking me up.'

'No bother.' He takes the case out of my hand. 'Better get a move on, I've the dog in the car.' He sets off ahead of me on his long legs.

Marty's a fast walker but a slow talker. He speaks in a townie drawl that makes him sound lethargic. At school, it earned him the nickname 'Shellakybooky'. But Marty was no snail. He was a champion sprinter who coached athletics for years. These days, he's more into walking, always with the dog. Walking and the dog are Marty's two passions in life, now that his knees are 'bet'.

The dog's breath is truly foul, so we drive down the motorway with the back windows open, shouting at each other to be heard. I tell Marty about the new terminal at Heathrow. He says it sounds much more civilized than the old one. I agree that it is, and he can't stop apologizing for the 'Buddy bang'.

'I'm afraid to leave him alone in the house with Tish, in case she poisons him.'

'How is she?' I ask.

'Holding up well,' he says. 'Given the way things are with Nancy.'

'Is she that bad?'

'Ah sure, it's a godforsaken hole that home. You'd lose the will to live.'

I feel the pinch of guilt as Marty tells me our mother's getting more hostile by the day.

'We're looking at a different nursing home,' he says. 'Tish will tell you all about it.'

My stomach does a flip at the prospect of that conversation.

In Kildare, we stop at a petrol station and Marty buys a fruit scone that crumbles and gets lodged in his new beard. He tells me there'll be a 24-hour service station on the motorway next time I come.

'With proper food: noodles, burgers and Subway sandwiches.'

I take a sip from my waxed coffee cup.

'They'll probably have Costa Coffee too,' he says. 'Or maybe even Lavazza.'

I've to stop myself from telling him I'd make the trip especially.

When we arrive in Tramore, Evie is playing hopscotch in the driveway. She dances around me as I take my bags from the boot, and Tish waves out the kitchen window at us. She has lost weight and her hair is in a short pixie cut that suits her.

'Did you hit traffic?' she says. 'I was expecting you sooner.'

I carry my bags to the guest room and Marty puts the dog into the garage. Tish pours wine for us, and Marty comes back carrying a six-pack of beer.

He opens one. '*Sláinte*,' he says, raising the bottle.

The table is already set, so we sit down to eat: coleslaw, rocket and cherry tomato salad, baked potatoes and a cold rotisserie chicken.

'Nothing fancy,' says Tish, 'compared to what you get in London.'

'It's perfect,' I say, suddenly remembering the bento box of salmon nigiri that I bought in Heathrow. I shoved it into my Duty Free bag and forgot about it. It's probably stinking out the guest room.

After dinner, I retrieve the sushi and discreetly put it into a bin in the garage, probably the wrong one. Then I return to the table with my gifts. They go down well, apart from Marty's cigarettes, of course. Tish opens another bottle, a New World Chardonnay, and Evie is dispatched to put on her Holy Communion dress. She does a twirl for me on the kitchen floor.

'Gorgeous,' I say, as she spins around in a flounce of organza and lace.

She collapses, dizzy and giggling, into my lap, and I notice her ears have been pierced.

'For the Communion,' Tish says.

I take out a lightning bolt stud and give it to Evie. 'You can wear one, and I'll wear the other, and that's how we'll remember each other when I go back to London.'

Tish sighs. I glance over at her. She looks depressed.

Marty asks if I've any plans for Tramore.

'Nah,' I say. 'I'm all yours.' Then, half to make conversation, half out of curiosity, I ask Tish if she remembers Helen Grant.

'Doesn't ring a bell.'

'She lived in Riverstown?'

'In the estate?'

'Yeah, we used to hang out together. She was always taking pictures?'

'Vaguely. Why?'

'I googled her and all that came up was a closed Facebook account. Do you think she still lives in Tramore?'

'Couldn't tell you.'

'I suppose I could call down to the house and ask her parents.'

Tish gets up suddenly from the table and tells Evie it's time for her bath. I take this as my cue to clear the dishes.

'Leave it,' she says to me, 'you don't know where anything goes.'

Next morning, I head down to the Prom with Evie. It's a dull day, the sky and sea are the same flat grey, the tide's in and there's nobody on the beach. We stand at the skate park railings and watch kids on stunt scooters fly up and down the ramps. We lick our 99s, and Evie tells me she's not allowed to get a scooter.

'Why not?'

'In case I fall and cut myself,' she says.

'I was forever falling when I was your age.'

'Were you?'

'Every single day.'

'Did my mammy ever fall?'

'Your mammy could hardly stand up straight,' I say, and Evie laughs. If she repeats this, Tish will go crazy.

We walk down the Prom to the arcades. Evie yanks the slot machine arm and squeals whenever it stops on three of a kind. At the far end, an old biddy in slippers and a thrift store cardigan is feeding her state pension into a poker machine. Between games she sticks her hand into a plastic bag, pulls out a naggin of vodka and takes a furtive gulp. Her skin is the colour of pastrami. She looks familiar, this dipso bag lady. I can't place her. I'm not sure I even want to.

Everyone's a winner!

Place your bets!

On your marks! Get set! Go!

The electronic blare is starting to get to me. By now, our machine has spewed out more than a hundred tickets. Evie rolls them into a bundle that she carries to the counter and exchanges for a fidget spinner.

'Can I have another go?' she says.

'A go on what?'

She points to the claw machine.

'That's a complete waste of money.'

'Please,' she whines, 'there's a unicorn –'

'No, Evie. We've been here long enough.'

She gives me the bottom lip, an expression that registers midway between heartache and fury.

In the end, I cajole her into leaving with the promise of a go on the waltzer. She sulks the whole way to the amusement park, but then comes around, and is bouncing up and down by the time the bell clangs for our ride to start. Being spun around at high velocity is less fun than I remember, and the *doof-doof-untz-untz* pouring out the six-foot speakers competes with Evie's screams to melt my brain. I mime to the teenager spinning our car that I'm going to throw up. He leaves us alone, but I'm still dizzy when the ride ends. Pleading for one more go on something, Evie drags me over to the pedalo pond, where they remove her sandals, zip her into a giant hamster ball, and launch her on to the water. I sit on a bench and smoke a cigarette. When they return her to me, it's almost time for lunch, so we get a takeout and walk home quickly, before our fish and chips go cold.

'You're late,' Tish says, opening the door. 'And I've already made sandwiches.'

'Sorry.'

'Marty will drive you to see Mam this afternoon, before he takes the dog for a walk.'

'That's great. Thanks.'

'You should've gone early. She's more coherent in the morning.'

Of course, Tish is right. When I arrive at the home, Nancy is asleep. I sit down quietly as possible beside the bed and put my phone on silent, for fear of waking her. Even before she lost her mind, our mother had to be approached with caution, like a fairy-tale dragon. Now, if it wasn't for the occasional childish snore, you'd think she was dead, with her sunken cheeks and paper-thin skin. The nightdress they've put on her is, as she'd say herself, 'appalling'. Nancy only ever wore cotton pyjamas. I suppose incontinence is easier to manage in a nightdress, but did it have to be nylon?

She's still sleeping when Marty reappears. I don't think I've ever been so glad to see him. We go back to the house and I offer to babysit Evie so they can go out, but Tish has gone ahead and booked a table for the four of us in Caruso's.

'C'mon,' I say. 'You never go out for dinner, just the two of you. Date night.'

'We see each other all the time.'

'It's not the same.'

'Did you come all the way from London to babysit?'

'No, but –'

'Besides, there's stuff we need to talk about.'

Tish is on her second glass of Chianti when she assails me over Nancy. 'You should've gone this morning. I told you she sleeps all afternoon.'

'Yeah, but I wanted to hang out with Evie on the beach.'

'The tide was in. You knew the tide would be in.'

I agree with her. It was a shame I hadn't spoken to our mother. 'I'll go back in the morning, if Marty doesn't mind, on the way to the airport.'

'Of course, he doesn't mind!'

Marty, squinting at the blackboard menu, begins to read the specials.

'Gorgonzola and walnut ravioli, osso bucco with saffron risotto and gremolata . . .'

'Isn't that veal?' Tish says.

'Yes,' I say. 'Sounds delicious.'

She snaps her menu shut. 'I think it's cruel.'

Marty orders 'the finest steak in Ireland', with rosemary and garlic potatoes. Tish orders pollo alla Milanese. I share a pizza Quattro Stagioni with Evie.

Why does everything have to be so difficult?

Outside, the sun is setting in layers of pink and gold over Tramore Bay. It's postcard perfect. I should love coming back to this place, but I don't. People never change, and I don't have the courage to walk away from them, not completely.

'Stella?' Tish says. 'Are you okay?'

I blow my nose into my paper napkin. 'I'm fine.'

'You don't look fine,' she says.

'It's just tough, you know, seeing Nancy look so –'

'Old?'

'No, we all grow old. She just looks so . . . defeated.'

Tish sighs. 'There's a new nursing home near Carrick – the Belvista. I'll show you the brochure when we get home.'

I nod and blow my nose again.

'It's expensive.'

'It doesn't matter,' I say. 'We can afford it between us.'

'We can, of course,' says Marty. 'Now, who wants tiramisu? I'm telling you, Stella, you have to taste this. The owner, Oliver, makes it himself, and I swear to Christ, it's better than what you'd get in Italy. Isn't it, Tish?'

Silently we spoon cream into our mouths, and I consider how things have turned out for my sister. Martin Devine is a good husband and father. I think about our own father, and how I hardly knew him. And I think about our brother Michael, who inherited Daddy's weak heart and barely saw forty.

*

Back at the house, while Tish is putting Evie to bed, Marty and I stand on the patio smoking. He asks if I'm going to be alright. I tell him I'm a bit tipsy but I'll survive.

'You seem upset.'

'I was earlier. But y'know, it's Tish, not me, who has to live with it – day in, day out. No wonder she gets frustrated.'

'Her bark is worse than her bite.'

'Yeah,' I say. 'She's her mother's daughter.'

He doesn't respond.

I look up at him, and feel an unmistakable pull. I'm about to kiss him when he drops his cigarette down the drain and says, 'I'm away to bed.'

I cannot sleep, so I unpack and repack my suitcase. I watch make-up tutorials on my phone and buy something called a 'pore minimizer' for £35. In the end, I get out of bed, make myself a cup of tea, creep outside, and smoke three cigarettes in a row, waiting for first light so I can walk along the Doneraile, and look out over the sea.

It's such a beautiful morning, I carry on down the hill and on to the Ladies' Slip. From here, the beach stretches out before me in open invitation and I walk the three-mile length of it. By the time I get back to the house, Tish has a full Irish on the go and she's in a chatty mood. Moving Nancy to the Belvista home is a game changer. I listen as she lists off all the reasons our mother will be better off there.

After a few rounds of hopscotch with Evie, it's time to go. My flight is at three, and we've to stop at the home on the way. I'm standing in the driveway, exchanging the kind of small talk that's a precursor to leaving, when Tish tells me she's remembered something about Helen Grant.

'What?'

'She's a wedding photographer.'

'Really? How do you know?'

'She did an album for a girl I work with. Black and white. Not my kind of thing, but it was well done, to be fair.'

'So, she's still in Tramore?'

'No, she's in Waterford. Lovestruck Photography, on the quay.'

'Why didn't you say?'

'I didn't want to tell you in front of Evie.'

'Why not?'

'The thing is, Stella . . . her father, I heard that he –'

'He what?'

'Well, he hung himself a while back.'

The full Irish gurgles inside me.

'And I heard it was Helen who found him.'

With that, Evie comes sprinting across the lawn. She wraps her arms around my middle and squeezes me with all her might.

'Safe travels,' says Tish, and she hugs me like she's afraid I might snap in half. Marty's waiting in the car, he's put my case in the boot, and the dog is pacing impatiently on the back seat. I get in and wave goodbye to my sister and my niece as we reverse out on to the road.

'Lie down,' Marty says to the dog. 'I can't see a thing with your stupid head.'

The dog barks, and keeps on barking until we pass the turn-off for the beach.

'Sorry about that. He thinks he's going for a walk.'

'Do you mind if I smoke?'

Marty takes a box of Marlboro Lights from the door well and passes them to me. 'Knock yourself out.'

As we drive along the ring road, I try to remember what Helen looked like. Dark, with intense eyes, and she was tall, like her father. He gave her a camera, one Christmas. I remember feeling jealous because she had a dad, and I didn't. Her father was cool, but at the end of it all, he hung himself. It was funny how Helen and I never stayed in touch. Maybe I'd look her up when I was back next. What would we have to talk about now? And what could I say about her father? Sorry for your trouble?

We cross the Suir River Bridge and beneath us the sludge-green water moves slowly towards the sea. I watch it through the steel cables and realize that I can't face my mother. Not this time.

'Marty,' I say. 'Do you think we could give the home a miss?'

'Really?'

'I'd like to go straight to the airport.'

'Are you sure?'

'Yes.'

Neither of us speaks for a while.

Once we're on the motorway, Marty flicks the stereo on. 'Do you know,' he says, 'what my guilty pleasure is?'

'Nope.'

'True crime podcasts.'

'Seriously?'

'Dead serious. I could drive all day on a good one.'

I turn my head to look at him. 'Please don't tell Tish that I didn't go.'

Without taking his eyes off the road, he finds my hand and gives it a little squeeze. 'Don't worry, Stella,' he says. 'You have my word.'

All Shook Up

Christy

Zuzanna didn't show up for work. For fuck's sake, it wasn't a big deal, a miscommunication was all. Who did she think was going to work the espresso machine now? Whenever Christy went near the contraption he scalded himself, and he hadn't a head on him this morning to be dealing with it. Was a cup of coffee too much to ask for? He winced as he banged the porta-filter one, two, three times until a perfect little cake of espresso fell out on to the drip tray. It looked like a block of hash. He sent her another text.

— Are you coming in today?

If she didn't, he might have to give her the sack, and if he got rid of her he'd have to replace her, and if he replaced her he'd end up with some local girl, who'd a face like boiled ham, and a salty tongue to match it. He wanted Zuzanna back. No harm done, he'd tell her he'd got it wrong. Fuck it, he'd apologize.

— Hey, I'm sorry about last night. Misunderstanding.

That said, who could blame him for getting the wrong end of the stick? Those jeggings she wore, with a gold zipper running up the seam of her arse, and her peachy bum cheeks baiting him every time she bent over to empty the glasswasher or take a bottle from the fridge. He felt a stirring now, even with a head on him. You'd want to be dead not to. And didn't the little minx hang around after closing? Sipping alcopops and throwing come-hither eyes at him as she adjusted her bra strap, crossing and uncrossing her legs until she lost her balance on the bar stool. He'd to lean in to stop her from falling and smashing her skull on the floor tiles. Once he'd his arms around her, it felt natural to kiss the girl.

The Gaggia spluttered coffee all over the place, the threads were gone on the group head again. He ran in behind the bar and flicked the switch to off. If he called the suppliers, he'd be left on hold for customer service, and then he'd be bulling when they advised him to consult the barista manual. This was his last chance saloon: Barramundi on the Prom. Get your shit together, Christy. Put some tunes on, give the floor a slap of the mop, get the stools down off the bar – and if anyone asks, tell them the coffee machine is out of order. Have a cup of tea, proper Barry's tea, no charge, my shout. Christ, was he getting the horn again? Ah no, it was only the phone on vibrate in his pocket. He whipped it out. Marcus-fucken-Mackey.

– *How's de boss? ETA 6 bells. The King coming along 4 de ride. Ok with u?*

Marcus Mackey and Jimmy 'The King' Croke. What crime had he committed to get saddled with this pair of 24-carat cunts? Each day seemed to hand down a stiffer sentence than the one that went before. He'd the worst run of luck any man could reasonably be expected to endure. First the recession, then his bathroom business hit the wall. When he defaulted on the mortgage, the bank was quick to threaten repossession, and Deirdre wasn't far behind them looking for a separation. The puss on her, cribbing about how she thought she'd married 'a winner'. Didn't he know the price of orthodontics? The girls had inherited his gnarly gob, four rows of train tracks they'd need between them. Their older brother had gone without, but with the girls it was different.

Can't it wait till they're older? I haven't the money, Dee, you know that. She poked him in the 38-inch gut, the only thing he'd gained since they broke up. Find it, she said, as if the last of the Celtic tigers were gone into hiding, all he'd to do was track them down and flog them each a luxury bathroom with heated towel rails, a sunken jacuzzi, and floor-to-ceiling travertine. He'd never seen his wife look better. She'd gone blonde and was Tinder-dieting. His own hair was falling out but he'd cultivated a beard that was doing a good job of hiding the jowls where his jawline used to be. Gratitude for small mercies in the face of sufferance.

The boom would be back – everyone said so – and in the meantime, all he needed was a break. Between them, they hadn't a pot to piss in, but if Mackey and The King could convince the Chinaman to sign the lease on Barramundi, they'd be home dry.

Oh, Zuzanna, would you get your Polish arse in here.

Mackey

At the far end of town, Marcus Mackey settled into the black leather recliner, adjusted his balls to the left, and lit a fat joint. It'd taken fifteen minutes to wrangle Maurice Grant's chair out the hatchback of his car, even though it'd gone in easy enough. He hadn't the energy now to drag it as far as the shed, he might as well leave it out on the grass. Some view of the race-course from here, and you could see Brownstown Head beyond in the bay, blue sky draped above it. Jesus, but this was a grand comfortable chair. Stick a bit of gaffer tape over the holes and what more could you ask for? That Geraldine Halpin was some head-wrecker. If it wasn't 'get rid of the chair', it was 'fix the washing machine', and now she wanted rent receipts. As for the daughter, you'd think butter wouldn't melt in her mouth, and him only after selling her an eighth last Friday. Jailbait, that one.

He'd be raking it in, once Li got the lease on Barramundi sorted. The Chinaman had two grow houses on the go. This Carrick weed he was smoking was subtle enough. You could drive and you could play guitar on it. But the stuff out of Kilmeaden was lethal, psychoactive shit that made you trippy and paranoid. It was too fucking much. They'd have young ones throwing whiteys all over the shop, and the guards would be on to them. He'd have a word with Li tonight, now the place was up and running, thanks to Christy Grant and the Polski mickey-magnet he was after taking on. Grant was up to his bollix in debt, and he knew SFA about the bar trade. But so long as they drew a crowd from town, he'd be too busy counting beans to give a shit. He was an ignorant bastard, all the same, the way he didn't answer text messages, as if they weren't worth his while. His aul lad Maurice had been the same.

Mackey closed his eyes, cupped his balls and listened to the peal of the Angelus carried up from Holy Cross on the midsummer breeze. Below in the house, his mother would be slicing turnover for sandwiches. Scallions and ham. No, scallions, cheese and ham – with a good blob of salad cream – that's what he'd the munchies for. And a gallon of tea.

But hang on now, what was that *bang-bang* coming around the bend? The unmistakable sound of Jimmy 'The King', exhaust backfiring and the Enfield bucking beneath him, in protest at the laundered diesel he was forever poisoning it with. He'd some nose for the grub. A hound dog if ever there was one. He could stomach a pound of red lead if he got it, and Mammy was prone to giving it. The fucker wasn't due for another hour. He knew the plan: pick up the karaoke gear in Ferrybank and give head-the-ball his weed, pay a courtesy call to Li's massage parlour, then back to Tramore for the soundcheck. But it suited him to be there now, sitting at the kitchen table, shirt collar up, helmet-flattened quiff, and his arm outstretched as Mammy pours the tea, amber as early-morning piss, into his cup. Sometimes Marcus had to remind her that he wasn't actually The King. You know that Elvis is dead, Mammy? She'd look at him like he'd a screw loose, like pity was her middle name, and she'd say, 'Faith, sure everyone knows that, Marcus.'

The King

We're pulled in for petrol at Pickardstown when Mackey says to me: Well, boss, have you the playlist sorted for tonight? Kein problemo, I say. Wasn't I up half the night looking through the catalogue? Mackey's at the business end of the operation, and I'm what you might call *the talent*. I'll let you in on a trade secret now: the key to good karaoke is knowing how to whip the crowd up. They want to see you in character: gold sunglasses, rhinestone jumpsuit, the whole shebang. I give them that – and a bit of the ol' Tennessee tremolo. Start off easy: 'Rock-A-Hula Baby' and 'Don't Be Cruel' to get their feet tapping the whole way up to the bar. Once they've a few drinks to settle the nerves, that's when you hand over the mic.

The problem with Mackey is he's a frustrated musician. He plays in a wedding band. Sleepless Knights, they call themselves. The lad hasn't a bad voice, to give him his due. There's a touch of Tom Petty about it, but the only time he sings is if there's a young one he's got his eye on. And it's always the same number: 'Hotel California' by The Eagles. No wonder you can't get your hole, I'm forever telling him. This car of his is some gas guzzler, he's out there at the pump with the numbers ticking over good-o. I get out and tell him I'm going to the counter for a Quick Pick on the Lotto. Will you get us a packet of Rolos? Mackey says. No bother, boy, I say. Then I make a run for it, because if he catches up and sees me with the wallet out, I could wind up stung for his jalopy juice and all.

When we're back on the road, he says to me, would you start tonight with 'Jailhouse Rock'? He puts the pedal to the metal and we're pushing eighty, spraying dirt on to the roadside traders, on to their strawberries and their spuds. No way, I tell him. It's better to hold back on the big numbers. Keep me powder dry. It's easier on the hips too. Li has a young one who'll sort your hips out, he says. I want nothing to do with the Chinaman, but any word against him Mackey puts down to racism.

'I'm not racist.'

'Yeah, you fucken are.'

'I don't like him cos he's a bollix, not cos he's Oriental.'

'Ha!' says Mackey. 'There you go again.'

Time to change the record. I tell him they've found proof that Elvis was an Irishman. The fucker rolls his eyes, I catch him at it in the mirror. Takes me for a fool, he does. But on I go anyway.

'There's an auctioneer above in Dublin who has

court papers to prove that his great-, great-, etcetera, grandfather, William Presley, was run out of Wickla.'

'Is that a fact?'

'No joke. He got an awful hiding and he'd to emigrate to Louisiana.'

'In your dreams,' Mackey says.

'Swear to God, boy, I saw it on the news, the papers are going under the slammer next week.'

'The hammer,' he says. 'Going under the hammer, you fucking numpty.'

We're on The Mall now, stopped at Reginald's Tower.

'Let me out,' I say.

'Ah now, Jimmy, would you not come with me? A happy ending at Li's place, and a pint of cider in the sun?'

'Sayonara,' I tell him. 'I'll see you at the clock tower at a quarter past three.' And away I go to collect me jumpsuit from the dry cleaners.

Christy

That's that, then. It is what it is. Not a word from Zuzanna. I'm on my own, Happy Hour and all. I'd have cancelled the karaoke, but Li's come in to talk about the lease. What the Chinaman sees in Mackey is beyond me, but I suppose there's plenty lost in translation when it's a foreigner you're talking to. He's after insisting on giving me a dig out, on coming in behind the bar. Where's yer one Svetlana? he goes. Big leery head on him. I tell him her name is Zuzanna and she's not well tonight. The place is fucking slammed. Two hen parties rocked up for Happy Hour, spray tan and tiaras all round, then a gang of lads walked in, pricks first. Mackey's pulling pints of cider like we've an orchard out the back. Jimmy 'The King' is giving it socks in his 'Blue Suede Shoes', and down at the end of the bar, sucking it all up, is the Chinaman and his protégé, Little Li. I think we're home and dry on this one, lads.

'Grant!' Mackey roars at me. 'Would you go down-stairs and change the keg of Bulmers?'

I'm on my way back up the cellar steps, and what do I see when I open the trapdoor but Mackey laid out on the rubber floor mat. There's a fella straddling him and he's pounding the head off him. Fists the size of melons. I close the door, retreat to the storeroom and call the guards.

If I'd any sense, the thing to do at this point would be to stay down there, with the crates and the kegs, waiting for the guards to arrive. And a voice – let's call it the voice of self-preservation – is telling me to do just that. But I know Mackey is getting a hiding up above, and I feel a responsibility to bear witness to it. Propped against the ducting on the cold room wall is a hurley, signed by the Munster champions and taken down from above the bar because GAA wasn't in the plan for Barramundi on the Prom. I get a hold on it now and go up the cellar steps again.

The hens have flown the coop, and the stags are looking over the bar with their jaws hanging. The big fella is on Mackey's back now, has him by the ponytail, walloping his head off the floor. And there, dancing around the pair of them, trying to defuse the situation, is Zuzanna. She grabs and tugs at the fella's shirt, but he shakes her off like she's a rag doll. I tighten my grip on the hurley stick and let out a roar at your man. Zuzanna's eyes meet mine and the look on her face is one of pure desperation. She mouths 'sorry'. Maybe it wasn't 'sorry' at all, it might have been something else. Something to the effect of, 'See what you've done?' Or, 'You're only a streak of shit.'

We hear the sirens then, and the big fella jumps up, puts the boot into Mackey one last time, and away he goes, seven feet tall, a cube for a head, like the fucking Terminator, with little Zuzanna trotting in his wake. Blue lights flash through the windows, and out on the dance floor, Jimmy 'The King' is swinging his hips and warbling along to 'All Shook Up'. *Mmm-mm*, he goes. *Yay, yay.*

I turn my head to where Li was sitting, but the Chinaman is nowhere to be seen.

On the Air

Muriel Power had eight rooms. All of them were empty until the guest she'd assigned to the Yellow Room arrived, full of apologies and drink, shortly before midnight. He signed himself into the visitors' book as *Mr Vincent J. Phelan BAgSc (Hons)*. 'I'm over from England,' he said, neglecting to mention the public houses he'd visited along the way. Muriel gave him the room key and informed him a hot breakfast would be available from half past seven.

If fifty years in hospitality had taught her anything it was that guests valued their privacy. She came and went from her own quarters on the backstairs. It wouldn't occur to her to ask a guest their business, because their business was none of hers. Not that it stopped her from supposing; there was no harm in a bit of natural curiosity, once you kept it to yourself. She reckoned this Vincent J. galoot had come for Sinéad Phelan's wedding. He was the stamp of Tipp Phelan, beyond in Carrigavantry. The broad self-important gait of him. His ginger hair had yellowed with age and his nose was crimson with rosacea. She could well imagine the situation: Verona Phelan wouldn't have him in her house, and Tipp wouldn't put him in the caravan park for fear they'd never get rid of him.

He lifted his duffel bag off the floor. 'I'll take my breakfast at nine.'

Muriel watched his mud-splattered trouser legs ascend the stairs, feet encased in a pair of dirty runners with frayed laces, one of which had come undone. If he hadn't proper shoes with him, Verona would be within her rights, as mother of the bride, to run him from the chapel.

The following morning, when he hadn't come down by half past nine, Muriel put the breakfast meats away. She was smoking her one and only Silk Cut of the day and listening to Maggie Crowe on the wireless when the service bell rang. This was the problem with people who moved abroad, they came back expecting all Ireland to revolve around them. Well, he could go dance for himself until she finished her cigarette, and if after that he was mannerly, she might stretch to a fry.

On the wireless, Maggie Crowe needed to take an ad break. 'But stay tuned,' she said, 'there's a lot of unhappy people in Tramore this morning – and I'll be back to tell you why.'

'Faith, do,' said Muriel. The town was drunk on misery.

The service bell dinged. She poked her head around the kitchen door. Vincent J. Phelan had assigned himself a table and was armed with a knife and fork, ready to lay into whatever was put before him.

'You'll take a fry?'

'I will,' he said, 'and a pot of tea if you have it, missus.'

Missus! if you don't mind. She'd three rashers that were on the turn, but they'd do for him. The ignoramus.

Between the sizzle of the frying pan and the kettle on the boil, it was hard to catch what Maggie was saying on the radio. She'd a man on, a young man by the sounds of it, and she was reading to him an account of Tramore from a guide book. Muriel threw a few sausages on to the pan. She turned the volume dial on the wireless up full.

'A town with little to recommend itself. Do you think that's fair?'

'I think it's accurate.'

'Unloved and litter-strewn?'

'Yes.'

'Depressed?'

'Yes,' said the man, 'that was my impression of Tramore.'

Muriel stabbed the sausages with a fork. They let off a hiss and a spit and one of them burst as she nudged them over to make room for the rashers. It was true, the town had seen better days, nobody would deny that, but they didn't need some guide book announcing it to the world. It was no reflection on the locals, the man said, albeit that people had taken his review personally. And for that, he was sorry.

Muriel went to the fridge and took out a stick of black pudding. His lordship would be expecting black pudding – you couldn't get it abroad in England, not the real stuff, so they all went mad for it when they came home.

'How many people will buy this guide book?' Maggie Crowe wanted to know.

The man paused. 'Golly, I couldn't say for sure.'

Golly? What kind of a person says that? Golly gumdrops. A West Brit, no doubt. Muriel dropped the fork into the frying pan.

She knew him! She'd met him! He'd stayed with her, this guide book writer. He'd been her guest. 'Golly, Miss Power,' he'd said as they walked around the dining room and hall together, looking at her mammy's old pictures on the wall. Black and white postcards of the Prom and the dance halls, the Hydro salt- and seawater baths. A modern marvel, in their time. His whole face lit up. 'How interesting,' he'd said. And that was all the encouragement she'd needed to go on.

'Saltwater was a tonic for the chest, you see. Asthmatics, people with bronchitis, any weakness in the lung, doctors used send them to Tramore.'

'Golly!'

'Oh yes,' she'd told him. 'The man who designed the Hydro was a friend of Éamon de Valera.'

Beyond the kitchen door, the service bell sounded again. One impatient *ding*. Would you credit the arrogance of that man? A right cockalorum, and barely an arse in his trousers. She cracked an egg into the pan. The yolk ruptured and a bit of shell landed in the white. It was good enough for him.

Who was this now, coming on the air with Maggie? Oh Blessed Mother of the Divine, not Mulcahy the vet, an opportunist if ever there was one. A hundred pound he'd once charged her to put a sick cat down, when she hadn't the heart or the strength to get a bucket and drown it herself. A cat wasn't a luxury when you'd a guest house to run. Mammy'd always kept a mouser be-cause you'd be giving refunds with both hands if a guest caught sight of a mouse. And as for rats, a rat could close you down entirely. Make no mistake about it, Oscar Mulcahy was a sponger – he'd never done a day's work in his life – the vet practice, the seat on the County Council, every bit of it was handed down to him by his Blueshirt father. Now here he was, shooting off his mouth almighty on the radio.

'That review is a pure disgrace,' he said, 'an out-and-out hatchet job.'

'Speaking of jobs,' said Maggie, 'isn't the upkeep of the town your job?'

Oscar Mulcahy cleared a glob of phlegm from his throat. 'Tramore holds many fond memories for Irish families, it's loved by generations up and down, across the length and breadth of the country –'

'What about the litter? Why aren't there more bins on the Prom?'

'The Prom overlooks the finest beach in Ireland. There's world-class horse racing in Tramore. And-and-and,' Mulcahy stuttered, 'families with ch-children, enjoying themselves on the amusements –'

'Councillor,' she began again. 'The point here is

litter, poor lighting, a lack of amenities . . . the author has no complaint about people enjoying themselves.'

'With respect, Maggie, I didn't interrupt you. The man says the town is depressing, and I'm telling you he's out of order. That kind of snob-snob-snobbery is devastating to the local economy, at a time when –'

The service bell sounded again. More of a plea than a demand, this time. He must like his eggs soft. Muriel loaded the breakfast plate, and took off into the dining room with it. Vincent J. Phelan had a hungover puss on him.

'Have you toast?'

'The toaster is broke.'

He frowned at the plate. 'Have you brown sauce?'

'I don't,' she said, walking away from him and into the hall.

She'd have to be quick now at finding the local station's number. The man from the guide book was right. Maggie Crowe knew it. Even Oscar Mulcahy knew it, but he'd sooner die than back down. Tramore *was* depressed. Muriel was depressed. Who wouldn't be? At night, after the pubs closed, volunteers in hivisibility jackets patrolled the cliff tops on the lookout for jumpers. They'd a hard station. When someone is hell-bent on ending things, they get the job done, one way or another, and that's when you'd hear the *whump* of the coastguard helicopter. Sometimes in the middle of the night, Muriel looked out the top window and saw a cone of light scouring the bay. Some of the cliff volunteers had lost a loved one this way. Didn't

Maggie have one of them on her show only last month? The mother of a sixteen-year-old – a popular lad and a promising hurler. She couldn't for the life of her understand why he did it. God love the poor woman.

Muriel punched the station number into her mobile phone. There was a click and a recorded message, then another click, and finally, a voice, girlish and bright, said, 'Hello!'

She steadied herself. 'Is that *The Early Bird Show*?'

'That's right.'

'My name is Muriel Power.'

'And how can I help you today?'

'I'm the proprietor of the Stella Maris guest house in Tramore.'

'I see,' said the girl.

Muriel coughed a little to clear her throat. 'I want to be put on the air.'

Greetings from Tramore

Did you know Dad was a gambler? I remember you sitting on the carpet with a dummy in your mouth, watching *Grandstand* with us on a Saturday afternoon while Mam and Miriam did the shopping. The stench of fresh shite rising out the back of your nappy, and myself and the auld fella ignoring it. I'd be on the couch and he'd be in the armchair, riding it like Piggott. He'd whip the air with an invisible crop down the final straight. 'No, no,' he'd groan, 'not a photo finish,' as the jockeys passed the post in a rainbow flash of silks.

If his horse came in, he'd scoop a handful of coins from his trouser pocket. I'd look for the fifty pence, and snatch one before he'd time to change his mind, then I'd boot down the road to Dolly's for a quarter of Kola Kubes. Christ, Joey, but I held that coin so tight the corners marked my palm, long after I'd swapped it for a bag of hard-boiled sugar.

Our marriage counsellor keeps on at me to talk about Dad.

'He was a big gambler,' I say.

'I see.'

She doesn't see. She's just talking down the clock in her IKEA swivel chair. 'And how does that make you feel?'

'It makes me feel like my father was a gambler.'

Carmen shoots me a look.

'Write down your feelings,' the counsellor says, 'it'll help you work things out.'

By 'work things out', what the counsellor means is: why I haven't managed to get Carmen pregnant after eighteen months of trying. The latest theory is I lacked a positive male role model growing up. Result? I've no confidence in my own ability to raise a child. The counsellor says 'unresolved grief' causes impotence. Bullshit. The fact of the matter is, and I've science to back me up on this, I'm not shooting blanks. My sperm count and motility are grand. I found this out at a fertility clinic that charged a couple of hundred euro to examine a paper cup of jism I shot off in a room full of porn. It was also where I found out that Carmen had two (or was it three?) abortions with her ex, in Madrid. After a year of tests, the clinic emptied our savings account and sent us away with the reassurance that our baby-making machinery was in order. Carmen should keep a sex diary, they said.

'That's not normal,' I said.

Given that I'd never been complicit in either the abortion or birth of a child, Carmen was quick to plant the blame for our infertility on my doorstep. 'The problem is in your head, Patrick,' became her mantra. She was spinning it out, month after month, with every negative blue line, in that sing-song accent that used to turn me on. In the end, after a protracted spell of mucho arguing and zero fucking, during which she disappeared back to Spain for a fortnight, we wound up with this couples' counsellor who has Carmen convinced she's in for twins, once my chakras are unblocked and I get my head sorted. To get the counsellor off my back, I agreed to 'revisit a place that holds painful memories'.

'Some people find it helpful to put their thoughts in a letter –'

'Can I burn it afterwards?'

Carmen's face twisted with disapproval. It didn't look much different to Carmen having an orgasm.

And that, Joey, is how I've ended up back in Tramore. I'm ninety-nine per cent sure I'm staying in the same guest house as the one we were in, that summer. The Stella Maris. I got a good look at the landlady as she put a plate of eggs down for my breakfast. I remember her having a perm and glasses the size of saucers. That's not what she looks like now, but the mole is still there. Do you remember the hairy black mole on her cheek? And how it was all we could see when she caught us hiding in the hot press? Miriam was on the stairs cribbing to Mam because she couldn't find us. Remember how amazed we were that Mole Face didn't tell? She just winked at the pair of us, and closed the door.

When she cleared the table this morning, I thought she might ask what my business was, and I considered telling her that I was the boy with the metal detector. It was nearly thirty years ago, maybe she's forgotten? It's possible, I suppose.

The metal detector! Jesus, how excited were we when Dad pulled it out from the boot of the car?

Mam tutted. 'Where did you get that?' Her arms were loaded with beach towels and plastic buckets.

He held the metal detector up over his head. 'A fella gave it to me.'

'I don't doubt it,' Mam sniffed, and she took off down the slip towards the strand.

We jostled each other out of the way to get a hold of it. Feck sandcastles!

'It's only on loan,' Dad said. 'Mind it, and if you find any Spanish gold, I want a cut.'

Then he headed for the racecourse, and we followed Mam and Miriam down on to the sand.

They say there's an addiction gene. Back then, the only thing you could be addicted to was alcohol. Dad wasn't much of a drinker, so he wasn't an addict. I tell you, Joey, there's plenty of them around here today, and the racecourse isn't even open. I went down the strip and watched a bit of Sky Sports in a hotel by the arcades, the kind of flowery-curtained hole that could really get in on you. After a few pints, I decided to go look at the sea. For perspective. Or something.

In the alleyways between the arcades men were standing around smoking, a few feet apart, as if bad luck was contagious. What were they gambling on? Poker? Roulette? Electronic gee-gees? A lad of about twenty walked out of a casino and we same-stepped from right to left and back again, desperate to get out of each other's way. I looked up at him and he was crying. What was the point in going to the beach after that? I walked back to the guest house and went to bed.

There's not much action in Tramore at this time of year. The amusements are closed, there's a massive chain coiled around the entrance gate, and a padlock the size of my hand. At the far end of the Promenade there are cafés and surf shacks that weren't around in our time. I bought a coffee earlier and sat outside them, one eye on the tide, watching surfers in their wetsuits, dripping on the footpath and banging their heads from side to side like amphibious death metallers.

Remember the candy-striped lifeguard's hut? At the top of the slip? Great shards of paint are coming away from the walls, and all along the Prom the balustrades are rusted. With last night's full moon, waves crashed over the sea wall and dumped seaweed on to the road; it sits there in great slimy mounds. It's nobody's job to move it, so nobody does. I turned my back on the town and cut across a patch of wasteland, through scutch grass and on to the dunes. From here the beach turns rocky: boulders first, then smooth round stones of purple and blue. It's littered with scraps of twine, cider cans, and the occasional lobster pot or broken buoy. Among the pebbles, a piece of quartz caught my eye. It was white, with spidery pink veins. It reminded me of how I found a piece of red jasper the summer we were here.

*

The metal detector was heavier than we thought. When it ran out of juice, we left it on the shingle and went combing the beach for gemstones.

'Paddy, is this one?'

'No, Joey, that's a pebble.'

'What about this?'

'That's just a piece of flint.'

You kept on coming back with bits of stone and bottle tops, none of it amounting to treasure. But then you found the razor clam.

'Look, Paddy. Look!'

I ran my fingers up and down the long brown shell. It was perfect.

'What's inside?'

'Dunno,' I said.

'Maybe it's full of diamonds.'

'Don't be dense. Diamonds grow in mines. Pearls come from the sea.'

It was my idea to go diving for pearls. You were worried another kid would steal your shell, so you kept your hand clamped around it as we bounded into the waves. I remember, at one point, looking at the shore and thinking somebody had moved the metal detector. It seemed much farther away. Then the sand beneath me dipped, and the water was suddenly up to my oxters. I roared at you to stay where you were. I ploughed against the current and got to you, I grabbed your arm and hauled you towards the shore.

'The shell!' you bawled. 'I dropped my shell.'

A wave broke on top of us, and you slipped out of

my grip. When I found my feet again, I couldn't see you. The undertow had pulled us apart.

They say when you're terrified, your screams make no sound. I know this is true, because it happened to me as I ran down the beach towards the nearest family, a woman and her two daughters – one of them had hair the colour of nectarines. The mother looked at me and said, 'Oh no. Oh Jesus, no.' The girl with the nectarine hair buried her face in a towel and started to cry.

The next thing I remember, I was back in the guest house. Just me and Mole Face, sitting on a yellow settee. The metal detector was lying on the floor and she was holding my hand. There was a half-pint glass of milk on the table. She wanted me to drink it.

Then, Dad arrived.

I have no memory of driving home to Dublin. I barely remember being at your funeral. It occurs to me now that myself and Miriam must have been sedated to get us through that week. But to tell you the truth, the next two years of school were the worst. I was the lad whose brother had drowned. Grief is like leprosy. People don't have time for you, only sympathy. I couldn't wait to go to a secondary school where nobody had heard of Patrick and Joseph O'Donnell.

At the end of my first year, Mam went back to Limerick and brought Miriam to live with her. She hasn't said your name, or Dad's name, to me in twenty-five years. He lives in our old house in Kimmage. He has, to myself and Miriam's surprise, developed an interest in carpentry. Most Sundays, we go for a pint in McGarry's. You can take it he's still partial to the odd flutter, because when they closed the dog track in Harold's Cross he was fuming for a year.

On your anniversary, I take him to Mount Jerome and he says a prayer beside your grave. 'God bless you, Joey. You were a good lad. And I thank the Almighty for sparing Paddy. Lord have mercy on us all.'

The Reason I'm Calling

I'm at the dishwasher when Marty comes home and tells me Mam is dying, again. I've had enough of her one-foot-in-the-grave routine. Evie has an Irish dancing competition in the morning, she's stretched out on a bin liner in the conservatory waiting for the Fake Bake to set on her legs. I've a wig in curlers, and a Deirdre of the Sorrows dress steaming in the bathroom. Mam couldn't have picked a worse day to die.

'Do you want a glass of wine?' Marty says.

He knows if I don't get ten units of Cabernet down my throttle tonight, he'll have to find another way to pacify me. He might even get a ride, depending on the ratio of alcohol to cortisol sloshing around in my veins – that and the waxing gibbous of my menstrual moon.

'Thanks,' I say.

'It won't be long,' he says, as if we're waiting on a bus.

I slug the wine to stop myself from asking him to say it one more time with feeling. St Martin of Tramore, what would I do without him? He's been sent from the home, full of nurses' tea and Custard Creams, to deliver the bad news. Here's the thing: I'm not great when it comes to death. Marty is better. It pains him less to thank the staff, even though he knows they're not as sorry as they let on. It wouldn't do to mope when you're in the business of sympathetic nods and saying it like you mean it: *There was nothing more that could be done*. The Belvista residents are all on their last legs, Zimmer-framing towards the finishing line. It'll be a photo finish between Mam and Mrs Barron. That said, Terence Pim is looking shook. He has the potential to beat them to it. They'll go peacefully in the end, or so the nurses would have you believe.

These women – they're always women – make me feel useless, because I am not, and will never be, as good at looking after Mam. With their matter-of-fact kindness, they'd remind you of midwives in the way they present your blood-streaked baba as though they'd never laid eyes on anything more precious. It's the same when the time comes to dispense with your shit-stained mother. It sounds cruel, I know. But when you've been called to a person's deathbed half a dozen times, you can't help but wilt. It'd make no difference to Mam if she waited until Sunday to die, and Evie could go to the Feis.

I suppose I should be more grateful to Marty. His visits get me off the hook. Never mind that it's not his place to fluff her pillows. He's only her son-in-law, after all.

'You'd better call your sister,' he says.

I pour more wine, precisely because I'll have to ring

Stella. Three years younger and two stone lighter than me. No husband. No kids. She wasn't wearing any knickers, the last time I saw her. I know this because she announced it in front of Evie and Marty. We were eating pizza down in Caruso's. Evie giggled. Marty blushed, and I imagined what it might feel like to ram a fork into my sister's eyeball. Stella Swaine, with her tattoos and her piercings, moved to New York, and next thing we knew she was 'The Artist Known as StarSky', making a small fortune in design. These days, she's into street art and multi-media installations. There's always a rant involved. Fuck the patriarchy. Fuck the bourgeoisie. Fuck galleries. Or words to that effect. Some days, she's an artist. Others, she's a curator. A dose, is what she is.

It's nearly nine o'clock and it's the weekend. She'll be at some shindig in Shoreditch – a launch or an opening, with a DJ and a free bar. It always boils down to the same thing. I'll have to book her flight, because she's three Tubes from home and can't do it on her mobile. Marty will drive up to Dublin to collect her from the airport, because Stella, despite her hatred of privatization and sworn allegiance to the proletariat, can't hack public transport. She finds it almost, but not quite, as unbearable as I find her.

She answers on my third attempt. My name has come up on her phone, but she doesn't say it. She pauses for a moment, long enough for me to ascertain she's somewhere quiet; not a pub, or a party. I won't have to wait while she finds a quiet spot to talk. Stella sighs and I feel her breath in my ear.

'Hello?'

'It's Tish.'

'Oh,' she says. 'Is Mum alright?'

She'd taken to calling our mother 'Mum' while she was at college. I was surprised when Mam embraced this new title, as if it lifted her out of her small-town existence and dropped her somewhere more cosmopolitan. We were in thrall to Stella's itinerant lifestyle, notified, as we were, by postcards every time she moved on. New York. Buenos Aires, Mexico – which she pronounced 'Meh-hee-koh'. Before the current stretch in London, there was a residency at an artists' collective in Cuba. Mam wasn't gone on Meh-hee-koh. 'They'd take the eye out of your head, those Mexicans,' she said. The grounds for this bias were a mystery, our mother had never met anyone from Mexico. That said, it was a rare pleasure to witness the two of them lock horns. Stella slung her bindle over her shoulder and hooked it. A postcard arrived from Havana a few months later. 'Isn't that lovely?' Mam said, sticking it on the fridge door with a Tramore Taxis magnet. All was forgiven, but if you so much as mentioned Mexico, her lips retracted to a pinhole.

That was back when Mam used to self-medicate. She'd zip around the county in her Opel Corsa, buy a box of Solpadeine from every chemist on every main street, then drive home to Dunford's and have her

Tramadol prescription filled. She'd managed to find a doctor in Waterford who'd prescribe anything she wanted in return for his forty-euro consultation fee. A chancer who'd been run out of Dublin, I once saw him slinking into a massage parlour on the quays. What a creep. But Mam wouldn't hear a word said against him. They'd an addict's regard for one another, or so it seemed to me. When I tried to talk to Stella about it, she told me to lighten up. 'She's a grown woman, Tish. Everyone needs a vice.'

Meddling wasn't worth the trouble. Mam could be sour with you for weeks. 'What do you care!' she'd say, and hang up the phone. I was working, Evie was still a baby, and she was no help to me. 'My family's reared,' she'd say, when I called in to ask about her wonky hip and gammy leg, and to see if she needed anything from Tesco. By then, she'd traded in the Corsa for an automatic. It didn't last long. Six months, maybe, before I got a call to say she'd been in an accident. She'd lost control of her car on the Suir River Bridge; if it wasn't for the fact that she was a slow driver, she'd have smashed right through the barrier, killing herself and the toll booth operator. After that, Marty was on call to chauffeur her around.

Stella asks me if I'm still there. Where else would I be?

'I am,' I say. The wine sloshes from the bottle into my glass. I turn on the kitchen tap to make some noise.

'How bad is she?'

'Worse than the last time.'

'Do you think I should come home?'

'It's your call,' I say, and immediately wish I hadn't, because it gives her the opportunity to point out that I was the one who called.

'You wouldn't be phoning unless you thought it was serious,' she says.

Stella was getting settled in London when things started to go seriously wrong with Mam. I'd regale her on Google Hangouts about the latest 'Nancies', as we liked to call them – lapses of decorum that Mam was entitled to at her age. Neither of us admitting that, at sixty-eight, she was hardly ancient, albeit she'd outlived our father by almost thirty years. There were things I didn't divulge to Stella about our mother's unravelling dignity. For instance, the problem with her waterworks. The comedic possibilities of incontinence would have been irresistible to my sister. But Stella wasn't the one who had to strip the bed, and boil-wash the sheets. I bought a rubber mattress protector in Argos, an ugly yellow thing that was watertight and didn't rustle when Mam shifted in the night. Soon the leakages started to happen during the day. She destroyed the armchairs and her clothes. 'Back on the rag,' she'd say, and we'd laugh it off, as I doused the place in Milton and hoovered up the Shake 'n' Vac. Anything becomes normal, if you do it often enough.

'She's using incontinence pads like they're going out of fashion,' I'd say to Marty.

'It's all ahead of us,' he'd reply, as if 'it' was something to look forward to.

Exhausting as that was, it was bliss compared to her first nursing home – an antechamber to hell that stank of boiled cabbage. The tea was thick as stew, and the woman who pushed the food trolley didn't broker complaints. The nurses fed her little pink tablets and an ochre lozenge that looked like it could fell a horse. Mam had trouble getting it down. They could have drip-fed half the drugs into her, but that would've required monitoring and resources the public health system did not have. She developed bedsores and mouth ulcers. Her gums were so inflamed she could no longer wear her dentures, and with nobody to do her highlights, a tuft of white hair stood stiff as meringue on top of her head. She lost her temper often, and then she lost her mind.

'Stasia?' she'd croak when I'd walk into the room, and she'd mistake me for her dead sister.

I'd say, 'Yes, Nancy,' because I thought it was what she wanted to hear.

Then she'd lift me out of it with curses. She'd call me a bitch and a hoor's melt. Once, she roared at me to get out, that I was only a cunt. I'd be so upset, arriving home, Marty would have to remind me that I was not Stasia, and that my mother was demented.

'She still knows who Stella is,' I'd say.

'Her mind is gone,' he'd say, as if that explained why I was the one she'd forgotten.

The worse she got, the more information I withheld from my sister. Her arrival in Tramore puts work on me. Marty's airport shuttle is only the start. Stella lives on avocados and green tea. She reads the labels on every box and jar, sniffing out badness: palm oil, trans fats, and what have you. There are cliff walks, sea swims, and monologues on single-use plastic, throughout which my daughter trails her auntie, a little asteroid orbiting the sun.

I tell her that Evie has a Feis in the morning.

'Will you still go?'

'Probably not.'

Stella is six hundred kilometres away. Rarely has she been this close, yet somehow the distance between us feels hemispheric. We could cross mountains to reach each other, but in the end we'd screw up the rendezvous.

'Are you at home?' I ask.

'Yes,' she says, the *Dah!* of her computer starting up in the background.

I imagine her flat – 'the studio', she calls it. Books and cans of spray paint tossed about the place, her cowboy boots at the foot of an unmade bed, a kitchenette with a two-ring hob and an under-the-counter fridge. All it contains is a bottle of vodka and half a lemon. On a wobbly antique table, salvaged from a skip, or a flea market, sits her MacBook.

'I'm looking up flights,' she says, tapping the keyboard. 'Tomorrow morning?'

'Yeah, okay. Marty will pick you up at the airport.'

'Thanks, Tish,' she says, 'I'll text you the flight number.'

In the conservatory, Evie is watching kitten videos on Marty's phone. Her mud-brown legs are stuck to the bin liner.

'Up,' I say, tossing a pair of old pyjamas on to the cane sofa.

'I hate those,' she says, eyes glued to the screen.

'Phone off. Peejays on.'

The pyjamas are non-negotiable. I'm done with stained sheets.

Evie whines, 'It's not fair.'

'Life's not fair,' I tell her.

'Ma-am!'

Enter Marty.

He orders her up off the bin liner. 'Get dressed for bed, and I'll come watch the rest of the video with you.'

She stomps out of the room and he turns to me and asks if everything is sorted.

'I think so.'

He smiles and says I'm not to worry. He's there for me.

Ah but, here's the thing: my husband colludes with my sister. When our brother died in Canada, Marty agreed with Stella that there wasn't any point in telling Mam. Michael had already been cremated, and Winona, his wife, had scattered the ashes on Dakota Indian land. How the fuck would we explain *that* to

Mam? She'd lose whatever was left of her mind. Marty agreed.

There's no denying that he admires Stella, that she appeals to his arty side. The side of him that writes on the sly. There's often a notebook sticking out of his pocket when he heads for the Back Strand to walk the dog. He keeps a stack of these jotters in the cubby of his nightstand. When you open the drawer, it rattles with junk: loose change and pens, spent batteries that roll up and down, ATM receipts, and notes scribbled on wrinkled scraps of paper; words that mean nothing to me. *Glaucous. Grey plover. 363 lost souls.* A few years ago, *The Irish Times* published something he wrote about a migration of brent geese on the salt marshes. His interest in birdlife, the earnestness of it, shocked me.

'What are you interested in?' Stella once asked me.

We were on the magnolia walk in Mount Congreve, and I was pushing Evie's buggy. It had one soft tyre and I was trying to hold it steady over the bumps in the path so I wouldn't wake her.

'The usual stuff,' I said.

'Like what?' Her question circled me like a wasp.

'Gardening,' I said, eventually. 'I like gardens.'

'Hmm.' She gazed at the pink and white petals shooting out in great fragrant bouquets all around us. 'I didn't know that.'

Neither did I, until I'd said it.

After she went back to London, I began to plant flowers and shrubs, packing compost in around them, sprinkling them with water. Soon we had the makings of a garden. Marty laid a stone patio and we stuck a trampoline on the lawn for Evie. This time tomorrow, myself and Stella will sit out there in the fading light. We'll drink too much wine and talk about Mam in the past tense, as if she's been gone for years.

Woodbine

Nancy Swaine died in August. I was in the chemist's, when I heard the news. The old woman ahead of me said it to Richard Dunford, who shook his big bovine head and let out a sigh. 'I know,' the woman rasped, 'it's desperate sad.' Dunford took a bottle of Exputex down off the shelf and slipped it into a white paper bag. He put the bag on the counter and said he was sorry to hear about Mrs Swaine. The woman blessed herself and set off on a round of 'rest in peace' and 'Lord have mercy', a holy litany that could have escalated into a decade of the rosary if I hadn't stepped forward.

'I'm collecting a prescription for Kathleen Grant.'

The woman scowled at me. She'd a mouth like a cat's arse.

'If you don't mind. I'm parked in a wheelchair space.'

Dunford retreated into his dispensary. The old woman took her change off the counter and put it into the zippered compartment of a handbag she'd strapped across her dumpy little body. 'Indeed and I do mind,' she muttered.

Out the corner of my eye I watched her dawdle in front of the Yankee Candle display. She picked one up, wrestled with the glass stopper, gave up and put it back on the shelf. As the automatic doors slid open, she threw a dirty look in my direction, and shuffled away. Alone at last, I took out my phone, and searched the online death notices.

> **Swaine, Nancy (née Bastible)**: late of Doneraile Drive, Tramore. Peacefully in the care of the Belvista Nursing Home. Predeceased by her husband Patrick, son Michael, and sisters Stasia and Mary. Much loved mother of Patricia (Tish) and Stella. Will be sadly missed by her brother Eugene, her son-in-law Martin, granddaughters Autumn, Willow (Saskatchewan, Canada) and Evie, her loving nephews, nieces, extended family, neighbours and friends. May Nancy's kind and gentle soul rest in eternal peace.

My mother's jaw dropped when I told her about Mrs Swaine. We were sitting at the kitchen table and I was putting her tablets into their sorting box. Two pink and two white pills, daily. A round yellow one, every other day. Blue/brown capsule, once a week – on Friday.

'Was she not a young woman?'

'In her early seventies, I think.'

Mam chewed on her lip. 'That's young.'

'I suppose it is.'

'Did she marry late?'

'Must have.'

'When's the funeral?'

'Monday.'

'I take it you're going?'

'I've to work.'

She looked at me crooked. 'You have to go, Helen.'

'Says who?'

'You were great pals with her daughter.'

Were we great pals? I suppose we were, for a time. In the end, it was me who didn't reply when Stella sent a letter to say sorry, that she never meant to get me into trouble. I'd understand, if I knew her mother. She didn't know my mother either, and the ructions she caused in our house. I never told Mam why Dessie Fagan let me go from the supermarket, but she knew that Da knew the reason. The two of us were back in cahoots, up to our old tricks, keeping secrets from her. After Paws gave Da the sack, I left school and went to work on the checkouts in Darrers. Stella did her Leaving with the Ursulines and went away to college. What she did after that, I couldn't tell you for sure.

If she ever came back to visit, I never saw her. People always come back to Tramore. They build sandcastles on the beach with their kids and take them for a go on the amusements. They stand in mile-long queues for chips and 99s, anything to relive the best bits of their own childhoods. Others might come for Christmas, or for race week, and there's always a wedding or a funeral on the go. The more they drink, the more they talk, answering questions nobody asked about people they hardly knew in the first place. That's how I heard that Stella had been living in New York. Somebody's cousin bumped into her there and was nearly certain she got married and changed her name. It might've been loose talk, but it explained why I found nothing when I searched for her online.

So yes, I still thought about Stella Swaine. What I tried not to think about was how things might have turned out differently, if we'd stayed friends.

The last time I saw her mother was at the Coastguard Gallery, about five years ago. I'd a series of botanical paintings in a group exhibition, miniature watercolours inspired by the Japanese Gardens. I painted them on bamboo washi. It wasn't easy to keep the brushstrokes delicate and precise, but I was happy with how they turned out. The opening night was one of those evenings that people said was like being on the Continent. The sea gleamed and gulls circled in the sky above the bay, silent as kites. I was outside with Yewande, enjoying the view, when one of the other artists came looking for me; somebody was asking about my work. We left our wine glasses on the picnic table and went inside. There, beside my paintings, much older but with the same neat helmet of highlights, and still wearing pearls, stood Nancy Swaine.

'Which one of you is responsible for these?' she said.

I stared at her, dumbfounded. Yewande confirmed

that I was the artist. Mrs Swaine took a step closer to the wall and peered into the frames.

'Isn't the azalea beautiful? And the hydrangea too, I was never able to grow the pink, only the blue. The soil needs to be alkaline, you see.'

Yewande unleashed her most dazzling smile, and Mrs Swaine went on.

'Of course, I'm not really able for the garden any more. It's completely wild – and the cats! Don't get me started about cats! Doing their business under every shrub.'

'Which painting do you like the most?' Yewande asked.

I wanted to scream at her to stop humouring this awful woman. This spiteful, vindictive cow of a woman.

'Oh, I adore woodbine, definitely the woodbine –'

'It's not for sale.'

Yewande's patience gave way. 'Helen!'

Stella's mother prattled on with childish persistence. 'The problem with woodbine, it's a demon when it gets up under the facia boards and into the gutters.'

I told her to pour bleach on the roots, and went back outside to finish my wine.

A moment later, Yewande came marching down the path towards me, curls bouncing furiously. Like a black Medusa.

'What the fuck was that about?'

'What?'

219

'Why were you so rude to that woman?'

I shrugged and took a swig of wine.

'Do you know her?'

'Went to school with her daughter.'

I couldn't remember if I'd told Yewande about Stella. Maybe I had, when we first met, those nights you kiss for hours and talk non-stop about yourself, or the version of yourself the other person might fall in love with.

'So you go back to acting like a teenager?'

'I don't want anything of mine in her house.'

'I thought you wanted to sell your work.'

'I do, but not to her.'

'Grow up, Helen.'

'Grow up?'

'Yeah.' She folded her arms across her chest. 'If you're not going to take your art seriously, accept that you're a wedding photographer, and get on with it.'

'We wouldn't be together unless I was a *wedding photographer* – as you put it.'

This was true, I'd met Yewande at Sinéad Phelan's wedding; she did the make-up and I did the photos. We worked so well together that people now booked us as a team.

'I know,' she said. 'And there's nothing wrong with being a photographer.'

'I don't see anything wrong with it, *you're* the one who seems to think it's not good enough.'

'Helen, you're always complaining about it. Saying you should be an artist.'

'I am a fucking artist, what do you think we're arguing about? Flowers?'

'You don't have the courage to be an artist.'

'Forgive me, Yewande, if I don't take career guidance from a beautician. No disrespect.'

We slept with a Swaine-sized gulf between us, that night. Yewande's shoulders were high, her body rigid. I lay awake, looking at the dip of the sheet between her ribcage and her hip. I wanted to put my arm in there, to spoon her, pull her towards me. But I didn't.

The next day, I apologized. We carried on, kept doing weddings, scrapped about everything and nothing. Before the year was out, Yewande left. She hadn't the energy to fake Christmas as well as everything else.

I spent the morning of Nancy Swaine's funeral thinking about my father. He left a note asking for no religious service and no eulogy. His ashes are in a gilded brass urn that I keep in my studio. I'll never scatter them.

There are two churches and two cemeteries in Tramore; the one closest to where Stella lived used to have a fair congregation of Protestants. A sculptor called Walter Budd RHA is buried in the graveyard. He was born in the Georgian terrace opposite the church. The council put a blue plaque on the house. I used to imagine those top town Protestants enduring dampness and draughts with stoicism. Polishing their pastry forks. Grapefruit spoons. Fortified by a foreign Bible. These days, you'd rarely see a funeral there. The headstones are ancient and scabbed with lichen. Still, the church hall does a brisk trade, selling jam and nursery plants to shoppers of all faiths and none.

This is *not* where Stella's mother's funeral was. No. She wound up where most people do, in Holy Cross. I remember when Moll died, the place was crammed, more than two hundred people stood as Da and Christy shouldered her coffin out of the church. It was the only time I saw my father cry. I didn't realize they were tears of pride until I was sitting in the fourth pew at Nancy Swaine's funeral mass, with the chapel empty behind me. Whatever trouble the woman had caused me, it was no way for her to go. In poorly timed unison, we kneeled and stood, the incense bucket swung, and from deep within the bell tower came a sombre *bong, bong*. Stella's mother was carried out by men in undertakers' suits. At the rear of her coffin was a tall, bearded man – the only relation there to give a hand. In his wake came the older sister, Tish, and behind her Stella, thin as a liquorice stalk, with a lace mantilla covering her face. She was holding hands with a red-haired girl, who could have been her daughter.

We do not choose who we love, and I would not have chosen Stella Swaine, yet here I was, my insides heaving at the prospect of talking to her again. What was I supposed to do? Shake her hand? Mumble something about her troubles?

I found her in the portico, with the child still attached to her. She lifted the black lace, leaned in, and kissed my cheek. 'Helen,' she whispered, 'I was hoping you'd come.'

Her breath was soothing on my skin, flushed now with the realization that I was close to tears. The girl at the end of her arm wriggled.

'This is Evie, my favourite niece.' The child broke away. 'Also, my only niece.' Stella smiled, gap-toothed and sixteen again.

I felt my heart somersault. 'You've hardly changed at all.'

'Neither have you.'

'I'm sorry about your mother.'

'I'm sorry too, Helen.' She took my hand in hers. 'Don't cry – please. I can't do tears.'

Over her shoulder, people were waiting for the family to take up position behind the hearse.

She drew the mantilla down over her face. 'I'm leaving on Wednesday. Will you call into the house later? For a drink?'

Was it possible she'd forgotten I was never invited to their house? That I wasn't even sure where it was? I studied her face for some inkling and found I was still no better at reading her. 'Which house is it?'

'You're kidding, right?'

Only then did it dawn on me that Stella remembered things differently.

They were calling her away to walk with them to the cemetery. 'Please come.' Her fingers were cold in my hand. '*Woodbine* – it's on the gate,' she said, letting go of me.

I called after her to say I'd be there. Stella didn't turn around. She followed her mother on to the road, gravel crunching beneath the soles of her red and silver cowboy boots.

Acknowledgements

The people in this book are not real but the town of Tramore is. It took up residence in my imagination when I was a child and has refused to leave. It's a wonderful place that still gives me great joy. I owe thanks to the late William Trevor, whose story 'Honeymoon in Tramore' set me off on a flight of fancy, the result of which you're holding in your hand.

Some chapters appeared in draft form elsewhere: 'Kamikaze' was broadcast on RTÉ Radio One as part of the Francis MacManus Short Story Competition, and 'St Otteran's' was published in *Harper's Bazaar* as 'Visiting Hours'.

I'd like to thank my agent, Claire Wilson of Rogers, Coleridge and White, for asking to see more of my work and for believing in its worth until she found the home I wanted for it at Penguin Sandycove. Thank you to my editor at Sandycove, Patricia Deevy, for loving and despairing over my characters as much as I do, and also to Isabelle Hanrahan and Fíodhna Ní Ghríofa; to Shân Morley Jones at Penguin for her forensic attention to detail; to Charlotte Daniels and Alice Chandler for the beautiful cover artwork.

I am deeply grateful to The Arts Council of Ireland for supporting me while I wrote this book. Thank you also to everyone on the MFA in Creative Writing at

UCD, especially Anne Enright, Paul Perry and Paula McGrath, and to fellow writers Aoife Fitzpatrick, Sarah Gilmartin and Colin Walsh for their encouragement and feedback on early drafts; also to Cormac Kinsella for his sound advice, and to Lisa-Jane and Adrian Fitz-simon for their kindness. Thank you to my mentor David Butler and my writing group buddies: Laura Moffett, Rachael O'Brien, Eimear Kilcullen, Stephen McFadden, Kit Connolly, Regina Walsh and Catherine Joyce.

Finally, to my parents Maudie and Peter Flannery. *The Amusements* is dedicated to Senan who makes me smile every single day.